Pieces of Me

Pieces of Me

Darlene Ryan

VOID

ORCA BOOK PUBLISHERS

Library and Archives Canada Cataloguing in Publication

Ryan, Darlene, 1958-
Pieces of me / Darlene Ryan.

Issued also in electronic formats.
ISBN 978-1-4598-0080-9

I. Title.
PS8635.Y35P53 2012   JC813'.6   C2012-902219-5

First published in the United States, 2012
Library of Congress Control Number: 2012937567

Summary: Living on the streets, Maddie forms an unlikely family and finds
that it takes more than good intentions to make things work.

*Orca Book Publishers is dedicated to preserving the environment and has printed this book
on paper certified by the Forest Stewardship Council®.*

Orca Book Publishers gratefully acknowledges the support for its publishing
programs provided by the following agencies: the Government of Canada through
the Canada Book Fund and the Canada Council for the Arts, and the Province of British
Columbia through the BC Arts Council and the Book Publishing Tax Credit.

Design by Teresa Bubela
Cover photography by First Light

ORCA BOOK PUBLISHERS
PO Box 5626, Stn. B
Victoria, BC Canada
V8R 6S4

ORCA BOOK PUBLISHERS
PO Box 468
CUSTER, WA USA
98240-0468

www.orcabook.com
Printed and bound in Canada.

15 14 13 12 • 4 3 2 1

one

As soon as they started praying, I got up. I was only a couple of rows from the back, and I figured I could make it to the door and get out without anybody noticing. All I wanted was somewhere to sleep. Somewhere dry. Somewhere warm. But the bed wasn't free. It came with a price. The price was sitting through the service.

I'd almost left as soon as they said that. I didn't want to hear about the road to hell. Some days I was pretty sure I was already on it. I'd had enough of being told I was a sinner from my mother's new boyfriend, Evan. I knew my mother well enough to know that she hadn't found Jesus the way she told Evan she had, unless he was in the fourth aisle over at Payless. She played the game well. But that didn't mean I had to play, at all.

The third time Evan hit me, I left. Evan said God talked to him. I don't think he did. If God did talk to people, I didn't see how he would choose Evan, with his thin, bloodless lips and pinched face that never smiled. And I knew there was no way God would tell Evan to slap me across the mouth.

So I left, and I wasn't going back—not ever, because when Mom ruined things with Evan, and she would, there would be someone else. There was always someone else.

This preacher had the same angry look that Evan had. He was warning us that God could see our sin, that God knew what was in our hearts and that we should be afraid. All I could think was that if God knew what was in my heart, then he would know all I wanted was somewhere to sleep. And there wasn't anything sinful in that.

The preacher, on the other hand, seemed to have a dark place in his heart. Did he really think God didn't know that?

Maybe I could have tuned it all out if he hadn't started in on a small, dark-haired girl in the front row, urging her to confess her sins and turn from her debauched ways. He actually used the word *debauched*. I figured the girl was fourteen or fifteen, tops. How many debauched things could she have done that were truly her choice?

She started to cry. Her nose was running and she swiped at it with her sleeve.

I hadn't been in a church since I was maybe five, but the words to a song they had sung came into my head:

Jesus loves me! This I know,
For the Bible tells me so.

There wasn't any love in this place. The pastor had his hand on the girl's head, pushing down, holding her in the pew while he prayed for her sins to be forgiven in a voice that bounced around the room while she cried and hiccuped.

I knew I'd rather be cold than sit in the pew and watch. Couldn't anyone see that what that girl needed was somewhere safe to sleep and food in her stomach? Not to be made a fool of, like she was the entertainment before we all got to eat.

As I moved for the door, a woman came toward me, waving me back to my seat. Her face was pulled into a frown, two lines carved into the space between her eyes and two more like brackets around her mouth.

"Sit down!" she hissed.

I took a step backward, but only one. I didn't need this. What I needed was a warm, dry place to sleep. That's what everyone sitting in the pews needed. Somewhere to sleep. Something to eat. Not a lecture. Not judgment from people who knew nothing about our lives.

I stepped around the woman and pushed my way out the door. She didn't try to stop me. She didn't ask me where I was going, or if I even had anywhere to go.

I moved quickly along the front of the stone building, going by people who were headed the other way. I rounded the corner to the parking lot and stopped to catch my breath, dropping my backpack on the ground and leaning against the rough stonework.

"Holy Rollers get to you too?" a voice asked.

I looked around, one hand automatically pulling into a fist, the other folding around the jagged piece of broken beer bottle I carried in my pocket. The speaker was sitting at the bottom of a set of metal steps at the back of the building. Probably the fire escape, I realized. I'd seen him around. He had long legs in dark jeans, some kind of equally dark hooded jacket and shaggy hair poking out from a wool cap. He looked harmless, but that doesn't always mean anything.

"It's just not my thing," I said.

"Are they doing the 'you're all going to hell unless you repent' bit, or have they moved on to praying over some poor sinner who made the mistake of sitting in the front row?"

I couldn't tell if he was being sarcastic or not. "The last part."

He shook his head and stood up. I pushed off from the wall and began to ease the hand holding the shard of glass out of my pocket. He came a couple of steps closer to me and then stopped. "You hungry?" he asked.

"I'm okay," I said.

"I didn't ask if you're okay. I asked if you're hungry."

There were enough people around on the other side of the building that I figured I wasn't in any real danger from him.

If I screamed, someone would come to see what was going on, even if it was just because they were curious.

He held out both hands. "I'm not going to try anything," he said. "I'm just asking if you want something to eat. I know a place."

"What's the catch?"

"Well, I'm not going to try to smite the devil out of you, if that's what you're asking."

I could see that he was smiling.

"But you will have to walk a bit. Maybe fifteen minutes." He shoved his hands in the pockets of his jacket. "If it'll make you feel better, I can walk on one side of the street and you can walk on the other."

"So what is this place?" I asked. "If you're talking about Pax, they'll be full by now." Pax was the other shelter in town.

"I'm not talking about Pax," he said. "I know someone. He works in the kitchen over at the hotel. People send stuff back because it's not exactly how they wanted it, and it goes in the garbage. There's nothing wrong with it. He slips it to me. There's plenty. No strings, I swear."

I hesitated. I had that piece of glass in one pocket and a whistle hidden on a cord around my neck. It was probably stupid to go with him, but I was too tired, cold and hungry to care. I shrugged. "Okay."

He pointed toward the street. "This way."

We started down the sidewalk. It was bare and kind of dirty. Even though it was just the beginning of March, there was no snow left. "I know it's not very gentlemanly of me," he said, "but I'm going to let you walk on the outside, that way you're closest to the street." He tipped his head and smiled at me. "You know, in case you want to go screaming into the night."

He was keeping a couple of feet between us. "Why are you doing this?" I asked.

"Why shouldn't I?" he countered.

"Because nobody does something unless they're after something," I said.

"What were you after when you gave your scarf to that little girl at the clean station over at Pax House?"

I stopped walking. "You were spying on me?" I said.

He was a couple of steps in front of me. He swiveled around. "I watch people," he said. "Don't you?"

I did. It was a way to stay safe—to watch people, to try and figure out what they were going to do, so you could be ready. I'd figured that out long before I came to the street. "I didn't need the scarf," I finally mumbled.

He gave a half shrug. "And I don't need all the food I'll get. It's not like I can save it."

I blew out a breath. "Fine."

We fell into step again, walking in silence for a block. With his long legs, he walked quickly, but I didn't mind. I walked pretty fast myself. We cut across the street at the corner, and again he was careful to let me be on the outside and keep lots of space between us.

"What's your name?" I asked.

"You can call me Q."

For what, I wondered. Quincy? Quentin? Or maybe nothing. Lots of people didn't use their real names on the street.

"Quinn," he said, as though he'd been reading my mind. "But I prefer Q."

"I'm Maddie," I said.

I glanced sideways in time to catch him smiling at me.

"Nice to meet you, Maddie," he said.

We walked the rest of the way to the hotel in silence. The building stretched up into the dark night sky, and with all the lights on, the front looked to me more like something from a horror movie than a fancy hotel where people paid hundreds of dollars just to spend one night.

I followed Q around to the back. He pointed to what looked like a picnic shelter at the edge of the pavement. The sides were covered but both ends were open, and I could see three benches inside. "Wait for me there," he said.

"What is that?" I asked.

"Smoke shack," he said over his shoulder. "Nobody uses it."

I walked over to it, checking things out carefully to make sure no one was hiding anywhere. Turns out it was too well lit for that, and the only place to hide would have been under the benches. I sat down on the closest bench with my back to one of the side walls and set my backpack beside me.

Q banged on a heavy metal door, and when it opened, he disappeared inside. He came back out in maybe a minute, carrying a large brown paper bag. He straddled the bench across from me, setting the bag next to him. "You picked a good night to come," he said, unfolding the top of the bag. "Lots of picky, picky people." He handed me a clamshell takeout container. "You like lasagna?"

I could feel the heat coming through the bottom of the box. "Yeah, thanks," I said. He tossed me a napkin-wrapped roll. Inside were a plastic fork, knife and spoon.

The lasagna was hot, spicy and cheesy. It was so hot it burned my tongue, and it was so good I didn't care.

"Somebody sent this back?" I asked Q.

"Yeah, apparently the server forgot to mention there's spinach in it." He shook his head. "It's vegetable lasagna. What did they think was in it?" He took another bite and then held up one hand, fishing in his jacket for something with the other. I froze, ready to drop the Styrofoam box and bolt if I had to. Q pulled out a small, stubby bottle of water and held it out to me. It was icy cold, the outside wet with condensation.

After the lasagna, there was a slice of chocolate cake to share. "What's wrong with that?" I asked, leaning over to look at the cake covered in plastic on a paper plate.

"The frosting is smudged," Q said.

"Now I know you're lying."

He shook his head. "Swear to God—not the Holy Rollers version of God either—I'm not making it up."

"But that's such a waste," I said. I licked the last of the
tomato sauce off my fork and speared a bite of the cake.
That thing about "melts in your mouth"? It did. I'd never
eaten anything so good. It was creamy and chocolaty and
sweet, with a touch of dark-chocolate bitterness. I slid down
the bench a bit closer to Q and got another bite.

We took turns, a bite for him, a bite for me, until there
was nothing but a smear of frosting on the bottom of the
plate. Q held it out to me. "Here," he said. "No point in
wasting that."

I scraped every last bit of chocolate off the cardboard
and then licked the fork clean. I was pretty sure Q didn't
care about my table manners.

He pulled the top of the paper bag open again. It made
me think of one of those little cars at the circus that ends up
having about six or seven clowns stuffed inside. This time Q
took out a smaller brown bag and offered it to me.

I shook my head. "No thanks. I'm full."

"Take it," he said. "It's just biscuits—cheese ones, and
I think raisins, or maybe cranberry. They'd be okay for
breakfast."

"What are you going to have?"

He pulled out a second bag. "There's plenty."

I took the food, setting it next to me on the bench. "Does
this much get thrown out every night?" I asked.

"Pretty much," Q said as he gathered up our garbage.
"Sometimes less, sometimes more."

I rubbed my hands together. They were getting cold again. "But it's such a waste. There are people down there at the shelter that are hungry—children. Old people. Would it be so hard to take it down to them instead of just tossing it all in a Dumpster?"

Q stretched his long legs across the space between us. "Can't," he said.

"Why?"

"Health department rules. All this food was already served to someone. They can't give it to anyone else."

I folded my arms across my chest for warmth. "What? They figure people spit in it or something?"

"Sneezed on it. Breathed on it," Q said. He got up, walked over to a big Dumpster by the back wall of the hotel and stuffed our trash inside. He came back across the pavement, stopping at the open end of the smoking shelter. "You have anywhere to sleep tonight?"

Here it was. The catch. I should have known. I stood up. "I knew there was no such thing as a free lunch," I said. "Or a free dinner." I fumbled in the pocket of my jeans and pulled out the last five dollars I had. I held it out to Q along with the bag of biscuits. "Here," I said. "I'm not having sex with you."

Q took a step backward and held up one hand. "Whoa! Who said anything about sex?" he said.

"You did," I said.

"I asked you if you had somewhere to sleep. I didn't say you had to sleep with me."

I was still holding out the money and the bag.

"I'm not taking that," Q said. "I had way more food than I could eat. I just wanted to share it. That's all." He dropped his hand. "I'm not a whore, Maddie. I don't trade sex for lasagna or somewhere to sleep." He looked at me like I'd disappointed him in some way. Then he turned and started for the front of the building.

I felt like a piece of crap, standing there with my hand out offering him money. Still, he wouldn't have been the first guy who had expected sex because he shared a bite of his sandwich. I'd had enough close calls to know that. But Q really did seem different. I grabbed my pack and took off after him before I really even thought about it. I caught him just as he reached the sidewalk. "Q, I'm sorry," I said. "It's just that nobody does stuff like this unless they're trying to take advantage of you in some way. At least nobody I know."

"You do," he said. "I saw what you did after you gave that kid your scarf. I saw you give that old lady your sandwich."

I shifted uncomfortably from one foot to another. "I wasn't really hungry," I said softly.

He grinned. "Yeah, 'cause there's so much gourmet food out here."

I grinned back. "Caviar and champagne every night."

Q kicked an empty paper coffee cup and sent it skittering down the sidewalk. "Look Maddie, I don't have sex with people I don't know. It's not something that should be bought and sold. It's…it's a covenant between two people."

He made a face. "I sound like the Holy Rollers, don't I? 'Your body is a temple. Save yourself for marriage.'" His tone turned mocking.

"You don't sound anything like them," I said. "Trust me."

"I do," Q said. "And you can trust me, Maddie. I don't do the casual sex thing."

I nodded. "Okay."

He let out a breath. "Here's the deal. I have this car. It doesn't work so well, but it's good for sleeping in and keeping my stuff. There's a bunch of people with RVs and campers who stay the night in the lot at All-mart—the store doesn't care. I was there last night, and I'm going back. You can have the front seat. I swear I'm not going to try anything, but we can rig up some kind of wall between the front seat and the back, if it makes you feel better."

Last night, I'd slept in a half-built house, wrapped up in a blanket and insulation. The two nights before that, I'd been in an abandoned building downtown. I studied Q's face. His eyes met mine. They didn't slide off my face the way most people's did when they were lying.

If he tried anything, I was going to cut him up good with that piece of glass in my pocket, but for some reason I didn't think he would. "As long as you don't try to save me from my sins," I said.

"Did I forget to mention there will be a small service?" he joked as I fell into step beside him. "Just a little hellfire and damnation and a few hallelujahs."

"Well, if there's just a little, I guess that's okay," I said. I couldn't keep a straight face.

He caught my smile and gave me back one of his own. I'd forgotten how good it felt to just talk to someone. I hoped I wouldn't be sorry when tomorrow came.

two

I wasn't. Q and I walked up the hill to the All-mart. In the side parking lot, there were maybe eight or nine campers— a couple of big RVs, some fifth wheel trailers being pulled behind an SUV or a half-ton, and even an old camper van. There was a white Honda Civic in between the camper van and a huge brown RV. I figured the car belonged to the RV people, but Q headed across the parking lot toward the Civic. He unlocked the passenger side and then went around to the driver's door.

The inside of the car was a faded gray color, and it was very clean. "That seat goes all the way back," Q said. "I'd give you the back but I don't exactly fit over there."

I looked at the backseat. I was surprised Q's long legs even fit there. I'm five foot six inches, and I was guessing he was more than half a foot taller.

"I've got a blanket we can hang up between the front and the back to give you a little privacy," he said.

"You don't have to do that."

"I know," he said. He reached behind my seat and pulled up a large piece of folded cardboard. "This goes up against the windshield. It keeps a lot of the light out."

There were lights on in the RV next to us. "You parked here on purpose, didn't you?" I asked. "So it would look like your car went with that RV."

He nodded. "Yeah. I saw them this morning. I'm pretty sure they knew I slept in the car, but they were cool about it." He pointed over at the department store. "We can use the washroom in there right before they close. I'll get you a couple of blankets."

Q got three blankets from a box behind the backseat, stretched a cord between the two clothes hooks just behind the car doors and draped one of the blankets over it, dividing the car into two tiny halves.

"You don't have to do all this, Q," I said.

He climbed back into the front seat. "You didn't have to give that woman your sandwich," he said.

"Is that what you do?" I asked. "Go around rewarding people who don't want all their lunch?"

He held out both hands, palms up. "Busted."

"Seriously, why are you doing this?" I had one hand around my backpack and the other behind me on the door handle. I could be gone in seconds, if I needed to.

Q leaned his head back against the headrest. "You're right, you know," he said.

"About what?"

"There's an awful lot of people who are just out for what they can get. And they're not all on the street. Sometimes I just want to be around someone who's not that way." He turned his head to look at me. "That's all, Maddie." He stared out the windshield. The silence spread around us, but it wasn't uncomfortable.

"How long have you been on your own?" I said finally.

He didn't answer right away, and I wasn't sure he'd even heard me. "Months," he said after awhile. "I kinda lose track. What about you?"

I shifted the bag on my lap. "A few weeks."

"What's your plan?" He turned his head back toward me again. "You don't have to tell me if you don't want to."

I leaned back in the seat. "I don't know exactly. Get some money. Get a room. Get a job, maybe go back to school."

He nodded, like that sounded good to him.

"What about you?"

He reached up and pulled off the knit cap, running both hands through his dark, curly hair. "Pretty much like you. Get some money. Only I want to live in the country, grow my own food. Be independent."

"That sounds good," I said.

He tossed the hat up onto the dash. "Yeah. Feels like a long way away sometimes, though." He sat up abruptly and reached between the seats into the back, grabbing something off the floor.

"What is that?" I said. It looked like a cross between a flashlight and one of those hand-crank food processors they advertised on late-night infomercials.

"It's a radio," Q said. "Hand-powered." He turned the handle, and it made a faint whirring sound. After he'd cranked it for a minute or so, he adjusted the volume and set the radio up next to his hat. "Is oldies stuff okay?" he asked. "It's the only station I can get here."

"Very okay," I said. My dad had loved old rock 'n' roll music. He died when I was six, but it made me feel closer to him when I heard any of those old songs.

Q and I listened to the radio, taking turns cranking the handle. About nine thirty, we went into the mall to use the washrooms. I brushed my teeth and waited until no one else was around to wash my face. Then I stared at my reflection in the wide mirror. Was I crazy spending the night with a guy I didn't know in a tiny Honda Civic? Except Q didn't feel like a stranger. I'd slept in worse places, I reminded the face looking back at me. And it was only for one night.

I pulled the elastic out of my hair and brushed it loose around my shoulders. And I didn't look at myself anymore.

Back in the car, Q showed me how to tip the seat back. "Are you sure you'll have enough room?" I asked.

He patted one thigh. "Oh yeah. Didn't I tell you? These things come off at night. I just fold them up into their own convenient carrying case." His lips were twitching.

I punched him lightly on the arm. "I'm serious."

He let the smile loose. "Yes, Maddie, I have enough room." He got out the driver's door, tipped the seat forward and climbed into the backseat, pulling the car door shut behind him.

I got the one blanket I had out of my backpack and wrapped myself up in it and the other two Q had given me. I could hear him moving around in the backseat.

"Did you lock your door?" he asked.

I felt behind me to check. "Yes," I said. There was more movement, then nothing. I stretched out in the seat. It was a lot more comfortable than I'd expected, a lot better than a filthy floor in an old building, that was for sure, and with the cardboard screen covering the windshield and the blanket wall between the front and backseat, it felt kind of cozy. I didn't want to think about it, but it almost felt...safe.

"Good night, Maddie," Q whispered from the backseat.

"Good night," I whispered back.

The light coming through the side window of the car woke me up. I sat up, letting the blankets fall, and stretched.

"Maddie, are you awake?" Q said quietly.

"Yes."

He pushed the blanket aside and poked his head around. "How did you sleep?"

"Good," I said. Considering I'd been sleeping in the front seat of a car, I had. I was warm, and it had been quiet. Nothing with more than two legs had crawled over me in the night—no bugs, no rats.

"Mall washrooms open at seven," Q said. "Bring your stuff, it's almost that now."

We used the bathrooms at the far end of the mall. There were maybe a couple of dozen people walking a circuit in the building. Some kind of exercise group, I guessed.

Q was waiting for me in front of a store that sold video games. "Wanna split a cup of coffee and have some breakfast?" he asked. He pointed to a set of double doors at the end of the mall. "If we go out those doors, there's a Tim's just around the corner."

I didn't have anywhere else to go. "Okay," I said. "But I have some change. I'm buying."

He tipped his head to the side and grinned at me as we started walking down to the doors.

"Yeah, I know, splitting a cup of coffee with you doesn't mean you're going to sleep with me," I said, keeping my face serious.

"You'd have to at least buy me a donut," he said with an equally straight face.

I bumped him with my backpack, and he laughed.

We got a large Double-Double and walked back to the car with it, passing the paper cup back and forth the way we'd shared the cake the night before. We ate the cheese biscuits from both of our bags, and I split a banana I had in my backpack.

After breakfast, I shook out my blanket and then rolled it up and stuffed it back in my pack.

"So what are you going to do?" Q asked.

I pulled an elastic off my arm and put my hair into a ponytail again. "I don't know," I said. "Probably go to the library for a while and then go over to Pax and see if I can have a shower." I didn't mention that I'd kind of gotten to be friends with Hannah, who ran the Pax shelter, and that she'd let me in to get cleaned up even before people started lining up for the hygiene bays. I tried not to take advantage of Hannah. And I didn't stay at Pax House very much. Hannah was always gently trying to persuade me to go home. Or at least call home. She couldn't conceive of a mother who cared more about herself than her kid.

"Why don't you stay here again tonight?" Q said as he brushed biscuit crumbs off the front of the heavy blue sweater he had changed into.

"I can't."

"Why? Is the atmosphere at Chez Abandoned Building better than this?"

"Because...because..." I didn't know what to say. Because I felt like I was using him? Because a part of me was still waiting for there to be a catch?

He slid his fingers along the top curve of the steering wheel. "I'm not trying to pressure you, Maddie." His eyes shifted sideways. "Okay, I am. It's just that I liked having someone to eat with, and I liked knowing I wasn't alone last night. And I knew I wasn't going to wake up in the middle of the night with a knife at my throat."

He took a deep breath and let it out. "Why don't we team up, just for a while, until we each get some money and we can go on with our plans?"

"You don't even know me," I said, fiddling with the zipper on the backpack.

"I know all I need to know," Q said. "What have I got to lose?"

"What have you got to gain?"

"Company."

"Uh-uh." I gave my head a quick shake. "I have to do more than that. I mean, if I did decide to, you know, hang around."

"Laundry," Q said.

"Laundry?"

"Yeah." He pulled the sleeve of his shirt down below the cuff of the blue sweater. The shirt was pink.

"Pretty," I said. I wasn't sure what he was getting at.

"It's not supposed to be pretty, Maddie," he said, stuffing the material back up his arm again. "It's supposed to be white."

I laughed.

"See? My laundry ability is laughable. You help with my wash, and that'll more than make up for sleeping in that seat and some lasagna that's going to go into the garbage otherwise. Please." He pressed both hands together and looked at me over the top of his fingers. "Pink is not my color."

I probably should have said no. But I didn't. "Okay," I said. "For a while. To see how it works."

Q dropped his hands. "Good," he said. "I'm going to have to move the car today because the RV people are moving on. But I think I have a couple of days' work lined up, cleaning out an old warehouse, and we might be able to park there for two or three nights. Can you meet me back here about six?"

It meant walking down the hill and back up again, but that wasn't really a big deal. "Six," I said. "I'll be over there by the doors, under the big A."

Q handed me the paper bag that still had two raisin biscuits in it. "Lunch," he said.

I stuffed it in the top of my backpack and looked around to make sure I had everything. "Okay, so I'll see you later," I said, reaching for the door handle.

"I'll be here, Maddie," he said.

I nodded and got out of the car. All the way down the hill, I kept asking myself what the heck I had gotten myself into. I'd spent the night with some guy I'd only known a few hours, and now I was going to hook my life to him? As I walked in the cool morning air, it didn't make quite as much sense as it had in the All-mart parking lot.

I told myself that just because I'd said I'd be there at six didn't mean I had to be. Then it hit me that it didn't mean Q had to be either.

three

I had an hour before the library opened, so I decided to walk over to Pax House and see if Hannah was there. She was just coming along the sidewalk as I turned the corner. She saw me and waited.

"Hi, Maddie. How are you?" she asked. She tried not to be too obvious as she checked me out, but I knew she was looking to see if I was clean and if I was getting skinnier. I stuffed both hands in my pockets. Hannah was a hugger, and I really wasn't. "I'm okay," I said.

"Do you have time for a visit?" she asked, shifting a canvas shopping bag from one hand to the other.

"Umm, yeah," I said. I reached for the shopping bag. "Let me take that."

Hannah smiled. "Thanks. It's heavy." I peeked in the top of the bag. "Potatoes," she said.

We walked around to the side door, which was for staff only. Hannah used her key to let us in. We put the potatoes in the kitchen, and then I followed Hannah down the hallway to her office. She put away her briefcase and then studied my face more closely. "Have you had breakfast?"

I nodded.

"How about some hot chocolate?" she asked.

"Sounds good," I said. I never turned down chocolate.

"I'll be right back."

She came back with a tall mug of cocoa for me with a marshmallow floating on top, and coffee for her. She pushed her glasses up her nose and leaned against the desk instead of going to sit in her desk chair, and I knew what that meant: the talk.

"I haven't seen you for a while. You haven't been coming here to sleep."

"I was over at St. Paul's," I said, bending my head over my cup to take a drink.

"Doesn't seem like your kind of place."

Hannah wasn't stupid, and she'd gotten to know me when I'd been staying at Pax and helping out wherever I could.

"It's okay," I said, licking marshmallow off the corner of my mouth.

Hannah took a long sip of her coffee. Something was going on behind the steadiness of her expression. "If you came back here, you might be able to go back to school," she said, casually.

There it was. I was the mouse, and school was a big piece of cheese, because Hannah knew how much I missed school. I hadn't made the mistake of letting anyone else know so much about me. "How?" I asked. "I don't have any records. I don't have a parent."

Hannah shrugged. "Those kinds of things can be handled," she said. "You could stay here for a while before you make the transition to somewhere else."

Somewhere else was back with my mom. Part of me kind of admired how Hannah wouldn't let go of the idea of Mom and me having a happy family reunion. You'd think, working in Pax House, she would have lost that fantasy about loving moms and happily ever after. But she hadn't. But part of me also felt pissed off because I just couldn't make Hannah let go of the idea of that happy ending for Mom and me. For one thing, I couldn't see how Evan was going to fit into that picture, assuming he was still around.

I took another drink of hot chocolate to buy some time. I wasn't going home. I wasn't calling my mom. If that meant I couldn't go to school right now, then that's just how it had to be. And I didn't want to tell that to Hannah for the four hundred and seventeenth time. "I'll think about it," I said, and I gave her a small fake smile over the top of my cup.

She smiled back, and I could tell that she thought she'd won some sort of victory. We talked about stuff that didn't matter after that. Pax House was going to be painted; a bunch of do-gooders from some community group were coming to do it over a weekend next month. The fact that it meant people would have nowhere to sleep for at least one night, probably two, hadn't seemed to occur to them. Or that the building had just been painted about six months ago. Painting the shelter was a way to say you were helping the homeless without actually going anywhere near the homeless. No smell of bodies that hadn't been washed in a month. No puke. No piss. No crazy people who talked to their invisible friends. Just cans of white paint that covered up all the things no one wanted to look at.

I didn't say any of that to Hannah. She would have told me I was too young to be so cynical.

Finally I stood up. "I should get going," I said. My face was starting to hurt from all the fake smiling and swallowing things I knew I shouldn't say.

"Do you want to use one of the hygiene bays before you go?" Hannah asked.

That was the whole reason I'd come there. I hated using the clean stations when there were a lot of people around. They didn't open until noon, but Hannah had let me in more than once in the morning. "Would it be okay?" I asked.

"Sure," she said. "C'mon."

I grabbed both cups so I could put them in the kitchen and followed her out. After she'd unlocked the door to the clean stations, Hannah wrapped me in a hug and I hugged her back, because even though I was never going to do what she wanted me to do, she was good to me, and I felt bad sometimes that I was never going to be who she wanted me to be.

"Think about school," she said, nudging her glasses up her nose again. "Come back in a couple of days and we'll talk more about it."

"Thank you, Hannah," I said.

I could see from the expression on her face that she thought that "thank you" meant that she'd convinced me. At least my face wasn't giving away that she hadn't.

There were rules stuck up everywhere in the hygiene bay. Rules over the lockers about not taking the key with you when you left. Rules on the wall behind the washers and dryers about how much soap to use and how to clean the lint filter.

On the door to each of the clean stations was a list of rules about their use. No food inside. No drugs. No alcohol. No sex inside the stations. And at the bottom, a reminder to remember the environment and conserve water. That one always made me laugh. Who uses fewer of the world's resources than homeless people?

I opened the doors to all the clean stations and picked the one that smelled the strongest of bleach cleaner. I locked the door, stashed my things and had a fast shower and washed my hair.

The hardest thing for me was keeping clean. I hated wearing my clothes for days at a time. I always secretly smelled myself to make sure I didn't stink.

I jammed my dirty clothes into a plastic bag I kept for that in my backpack. I didn't like doing my laundry at Pax. I'd rather scrounge for money and do it at the Laundromat. It was warm there, nobody bothered me, and I liked to read all those crazy confession magazines that always seemed to be lying around, with stories like "God Needed an Angel" and "Confessions of a Credit Card Junkie." My life didn't seem so bad in comparison.

I spent the rest of the day at the library. I read the newspaper, and after that I went back in the stacks and found the math book I was using to teach myself calculus. I felt a bit guilty about hiding the book. I would have borrowed it if I'd been able to have a library card, but you couldn't have one of those without an address and a phone number.

Q was standing under the big A when I came across the mall parking lot just before six. I'd argued with myself all the way up the hill about whether it was a good idea, but in the end, where the heck else did I have to go, other than back to Hannah at Pax House?

Q smiled when he caught sight of me, and I found myself smiling back. Then I gave myself a mental kick. This was only for a while. It would be bad to depend on Q too much or get used to having someone else around.

His hair was damp and combed back from his face. And something had put him in a good mood, because he was almost bouncing.

"Hey, Maddie, how was your day?" he asked as he led me across the pavement past people pushing carts toward the store.

"Okay," I said. "How was yours? You look like you ate jumping beans for lunch."

He laughed and ruffled his wet hair with one hand. "Actually I did have beans for lunch—with ham and brown bread."

I'd had the leftover biscuits and an apple. I felt a pinch of jealousy.

We zigzagged through two rows of parked cars, and then I saw the white Civic parked next to a huge suv. Q let me in on the passenger side and went around and got in the driver's door. "I have somewhere we can put the car for the next three or four nights, maybe as long as a week. Plus there's a bathroom and a stove that works."

I opened my mouth to ask him how much sneaking around and hiding from cops it was going to involve, but he did that mind-reading thing again and held up his hand. "And no breaking in anywhere."

"How did you manage that?" I asked. I held my backpack tight on my lap. If anything seemed off about Q's explanation, I was gone.

He pulled a water bottle from his pocket and held it out to me. I shook my head, so he unscrewed the top and took a long drink. "Remember I told you this morning I might have some work?"

"Yeah."

"Guy bought an old car dealership. He needs the inside pretty much gutted, and he doesn't want to hire union guys. So everyone's working off the books for cash." He screwed the cap back on the bottle and stuck it back in his pocket. "He was asking around after lunch if anyone was interested in being night watchman. I can pull the car in at the back of the building. There's a sink and toilet, and for now the stove works."

He twisted in his seat and pointed behind the mall. "It's just down at the end of Laird Road. And the best part? Guy has someone bring in lunch because it's a lot faster. There's still food left in the fridge, and we can have it."

"So why's this guy helping you out?" I hated how mean my voice sounded.

"He's not helping me out," Q said. "I'm helping him. Where else is he going to find someone who'll stay all night in a half-torn-to-hell building for fifty bucks and some beans?"

"So really, he's taking advantage of you?" I said.

Q pulled a hand over his chin, which was dark with stubble. "Yeah. And I'm taking advantage of him, so I think the universe will stay in balance." His eyes went from my face to my arms wrapped tightly around my pack. "What do you say, Maddie?" he asked. "Wanna loosen up that death grip on your bag and go get some beans?"

I could feel my cheeks getting red. I set the backpack on the floor at my feet. "Let's go," I said.

I was picturing something a lot messier and dirtier than what it was like when we got to the building. Q had a key to the double bay doors at the back. He got out to lift the door and told me to slide over.

"You know how to drive, right?" he said.

I knew how to drive. I just didn't have a license. Of course, I was just moving the car a few feet into the garage. I wasn't about to go barreling down the highway past that speed trap they always set up where the old tourism information center used to be.

"I can drive," I said.

"Okay, so when I get the door up, just pull in and park it close to the back wall."

I could do that. Couldn't I? I didn't say that out loud. I just nodded, and when the door rolled up, I drove smoothly in and stopped about three feet from the end wall, like I knew what I was doing.

Q made sure both bays were locked and then walked around the building to check that all the other doors were locked as well. I just followed behind him, being nosy. There was newspaper covering all the windows at the front of the building. There was nothing in the space other than dust.

Even the floor was gone, nothing under my feet but what looked like dirty concrete.

The back of the building was better. The bathroom was just a sink and a toilet, but it was reasonably clean. There were no top cupboards in the small kitchen, which I guessed had been some kind of staff room, but both the fridge and stove worked.

The best part was the office. It wasn't very big, but that was mostly because there was a desk, a dented black filing cabinet and two...two sofas.

Q came up behind me. "I think we can move the desk and the filing cabinet and we could each take a couch," he said. He stretched his arms over his head. "I know it wouldn't be a bed, but it's a heck of a lot closer to one than the car."

He was really tall—he had to be over six feet—and it struck me that the back of the Civic probably wasn't very comfortable. Of course, *comfortable* was a relative thing on the street.

The filing cabinet was the hardest to shift. "Are you sure no one's going to care that we moved this stuff around?" I asked.

Q wiped sweat off his forehead. "No one gives a shit about this stuff, Maddie. It's all going to the dump in a few days."

"But that's a waste," I said, running my hand over the seat of the couch. There were no rips in the black vinyl, no dents in the metal frame. The filing cabinet was kind of banged up, like maybe someone had kicked it a bunch of times, but the desk was nice—real wood.

"I know," Q said, leaning against the windowsill. "Hey, maybe we should take it."

"Sure," I said, wiping my sweaty hands on my jeans. "Put the two sofas in the back of the car and the filing cabinet on the seat. But what do we do with the desk?"

"Tie it to the roof."

I sat on the corner of the desk, laughing.

"I'm serious," Q said. "If I could borrow a truck, we could haul all this stuff to the resale shop and make a little money."

"Can you borrow a truck?"

He did a little drumbeat with both hands on the window ledge. "Maybe. There's a guy—Sam—who's working here. He's got this old truck. I'd have to at least get him a case of beer." He stood up. "Let me work on it. Are you hungry?"

I nodded.

We went back to the kitchen. There was ham, beans, crispy potato bites and even about a quarter of a bottle of root beer on the bottom shelf of the refrigerator. "Are you sure it's okay to eat this?" I asked Q. He gave me a look, kind of a half smile that I couldn't make sense of. "What?" I said.

"Nothing. I was just thinking if everyone was like you, the world would be a pretty great place."

"Like me?" I said, setting the foil takeout containers on the counter. "You think everyone should live on the street?"

He made a face. "That might not be such a bad idea. But no, what I meant was you always think about what effect your actions have on other people."

"You've only known me for a day," I said. "I'm not really that nice."

I thought he was going to say something flippant back, but he just smiled and said, "I think you are."

I heated the food in the oven. Two nights of good hot food. I was getting spoiled. After we'd eaten, Q gathered the garbage and took it out to the Dumpster at the back of the building. He came back with the blankets and the crank radio. We each took a sofa, and Q cranked the radio, setting it between us.

"What time do we have to be out of here in the morning?" I asked.

"Before seven," Q said. "Sorry."

"That's okay," I said. I studied the dusty ceiling tiles over my head, wondering if I was the first person to stretch out on this couch in this office.

"If you were serious about the laundry, I could take you there," Q said.

The Laundromat was good for a couple of hours, maybe more, if I stretched it. "I was serious," I said. "But what am I going to do with all the clean stuff when I'm done?" There was no way I could take a garbage bag full of clothes into the library, even if it was clean stuff.

"I didn't think about that," he muttered.

I let the silence hang there, and suddenly Q sat up and leaned around the filing cabinet. "I'll leave the car at the laundry place, and then I can walk or hitch back up here. It should be okay there. I'll come down at the end of the day and get it."

I rolled over onto my side. "No," I said. "You don't need to do that. I'll go get a locker over at Pax for the day." And if I timed it right, I might be able to avoid Hannah.

Q pulled a hand through his hair. "It's three blocks from the Laundromat to Pax."

"I've carried stuff a lot farther than that," I said.

"All right," he said. "But I'll pick you up there. You can't carry everything all the way up here. And we have to go over to the hotel anyway, because Kevin—you know, my buddy— he's working tomorrow night."

"Could you pick me up at the library?" I said. I didn't want Hannah to see me with Q. That would bring a whole new set of questions I didn't want to answer.

He shrugged. "Sure."

We lay there stretched out in silence for a while as the room got darker. Then Q said softly into the darkness, "You really are that nice, Maddie."

After another silence, Q started talking about the place he wanted in the country someday, a little house with solar panels and a wind generator so he could be independent.

"You want to grow your own vegetables and all that?"
I asked. Somehow it was easier to talk with the darkness all
around us.

"Yeah," he said. I could hear him shift around on the
sofa. "Last summer I worked on an organic farm. I didn't
know what carrots were supposed to taste like. Or tomatoes.
Everything really. And they didn't waste anything. Everything,
everybody had a purpose. I wanna live like that."

"It sounds nice," I said. It did, although it wasn't something I'd do.

"I even know where I'd go," he said. "All I need is the
money." He reached over to crank the radio again. "Have
you noticed people who say money can't buy happiness
always have money?"

Q's words made me think of my mother. She always said
people who said money can't buy happiness didn't know
where to shop.

I didn't want to think about her. I closed my eyes and
let the radio and the sound of Q's voice wrap themselves
around me.

four

It was cold in the morning. Q laughed when he caught me tidying up the kitchen. "Maddie, by lunchtime this is all going to be ripped out. Leave it."

I felt kind of stupid, but I just hated leaving a mess behind.

We stopped at Tim's on the way down the hill for a small coffee and a muffin each. I needed to figure out how to make some money. I couldn't live off of Q just for doing some laundry.

I managed to stretch my time in the Laundromat to more than two hours. I folded everything and stuffed it all in a black garbage bag. It wasn't heavy, but it was still slow going along the sidewalk to Pax House. I was a block away before I remembered that the hygiene bays didn't open for almost an hour, which meant I couldn't get a locker for an hour. I didn't want to stand around outside for that long. Hannah would see me and want to talk about school.

So I turned left at the corner and walked to the park. I found a bench in the sun and sat for a while, watching a crazy squirrel swipe sunflower seeds from a bird feeder in the front yard across the street and then hide them in the grass along the edge of the gravel path.

He'd make his way carefully along the thin branch where the feeder was and then hang upside down, holding on with his feet, and stuff his face with seeds. A couple of times he almost fell, but that didn't stop him.

There was a line forming outside the hygiene bay when I got back to Pax. I joined the end of it, holding the garbage bag with both arms so it blocked my face. In front of me was a mother with two little kids and a baby. The kids looked like they'd been eating okay, but the mother was thin. Only the baby seemed not to know where she was. She grinned at me, and I made faces back at her. When the line finally started moving, the mother glanced back at me and gave me a tired smile.

"Your baby's beautiful," I said.

"Thank you," she said. She herded the other children forward with one hand.

Like me, she was headed for the lockers. I put my four quarters in the slot, turned the key and pulled the door open. I had to jam the bag inside, pushing with my hip and elbows.

A couple of lockers away, I saw the mother press her hand to her mouth and close her eyes for a second. She bent down to the oldest child, a little boy who was carrying a plastic shopping bag. "I'm sorry," she said softly. "You have to put money in, and I don't have any."

The boy was holding the bag with two hands, and even so, it was almost dragging on the floor.

I moved over to them, bent down and swept my hand over the floor. "I think you dropped this." I held out my hand with four quarters.

She looked at me, confused. "I didn't drop anything," she said in her quiet voice.

I shrugged. "Well, whoever did isn't here, so you might as well use it for your locker." I dropped the money in the slot, turned the key and then handed it to her.

Her eyes went from the locker to the children to me. "Thank you," she whispered.

"You're welcome," I said. I smiled at the baby and wiggled my nose at her, which gave her a fit of giggles. It was a great sound.

There were a couple of clean stations free so I used the washroom, washed my face, quickly braided my hair, and brushed my teeth. When I stepped back outside, the mother and her kids were heading up the sidewalk. Watching them, I suddenly felt like there was a big rock sitting in the middle of my stomach. If I saw them again, maybe I'd point them out to Hannah. It would be worth another "talk" about going home.

I spent a bit more than an hour at the library working on math. I'd been going to skip lunch, but my stomach had other ideas. The two dollars I'd used for lockers was the last of my money other than my emergency fund. That meant if I wanted to eat, I'd have to go to the Community Kitchen. Most of the time I'd rather be hungry than go there, but today my head hurt and that made it hard to read the equations on the page. I didn't want it to turn into one of those pounding headaches that made me feel like someone was using my head for a drum with a baseball bat for a stick.

There were a lot of crazy people at the Community Kitchen. I wasn't being mean. It was a fact. Most of the mentally ill street people depended on that place to stay alive. I felt bad that they scared the crap out of me— it wasn't their fault that they were crazy and all.

The closer I got to the kitchen, the slower I walked. I kept thinking I should go back to the library or use a bit of my emergency money. I could see the line—there were only maybe a dozen people in it—when I got close to the building, and I knew I couldn't go stand in it. I'd rather be hungry. I'd rather have this headache for the rest of the day.

I was just turning around when I saw her—the mother with the kids and the baby. She was at the edge of the parking lot staring at the line. Crap. I knew from experience that anyone young in line was a magnet for crazies.

I took a deep breath and then another. All that did was make me feel like I was going to pass out. I felt for the cord holding the whistle around my neck. It was there. So was the piece of glass in my pocket. "Just go," I said softly. Then I had to laugh. I was talking to myself out loud. Who was the crazy now?

I walked over to them and touched the mother on the arm. She almost came out of her skin. "Hi," I said. "I'm sorry, I didn't mean to scare you."

"Oh, hello," she said. Her eyes slid off me, back to the line. The baby twisted in her mother's arms and grinned. She clearly remembered me.

"Are you going for lunch?" I asked. "Would you mind if I sit next to you? I just don't want to sit by myself."

She gave a slight nod. "I don't mind."

We walked across the parking lot and joined the end of the line. She kept the two older kids close to her side, one arm around them. I moved to the other side, at least partly shielding them from sight of the rest of the line.

There was the usual pushing as we began to move toward the door but no craziness. No one came up to me insisting bugs were coming out of my nose. No one yelled that I had taken his invisible friend's place in line.

Inside, I helped the kids with their trays and steered them all to a table in front, which was a better place to sit even if it was closer to the food line. We were about halfway through our meal—weirdly enough, lasagna, nothing like what I'd eaten from the hotel, although it was nice and hot— when an old man climbed onto his table by the back wall.

Maybe he wasn't that old. It was just that he looked so gray—gray hair, faded gray suit, even gray skin.

He started reciting something. It only took two lines for me to realize it was Shakespeare. His voice was deep, and it boomed off the walls of the small room. Since he wasn't causing a problem, the staff left him alone.

Almost everyone went on eating. The kids were looking at their mother wide-eyed. "He has a really loud voice, doesn't he?" I said to the little guy next to me. He nodded, but didn't say anything. "I'll tell you a secret," I continued. "It's so loud, it kind of scares me."

God knew that was the truth. Under the long table, my legs were shaking.

There was something about the look on the mom's face that made me think of a dog that thought you were about to hit it. I wanted to tell her to suck it up for her kids. Like I was any expert on mothers sucking it up for their children. And then she did. She plastered a smile on her face. "It's okay if you feel a little scared," she said to me. She looked at the little guy beside me and pointed to the man on the table. "He's just showing off, isn't he, Dylan?"

Dylan looked at me and nodded slowly. "He should be using his inside voice," he said, his forehead wrinkled in a frown.

"Some people forget that," his mother said.

"Not me." He straightened his shoulders proudly.

I leaned toward him. "I forget sometimes," I whispered.

He reached over and patted my hand. "That's okay," he said.

The other kids were already eating again. I picked up my fork, and so did Dylan.

There were just a few stragglers dragging in when we were finished. I looked over at the serving area. I could see that there were maybe a dozen cookies left. There was always something sweet here for dessert. Some of the people who came here had drug problems, and they always seemed to have a sweet tooth. I went over to the counter. The guy on the other side had arms that were bigger than my legs. I smiled at him.

"You think I could get a cookie for the little ones?" I asked. I pointed at the kids. Dylan was putting a coat on his younger brother, and his mother was getting the baby dressed.

"One per customer," he snapped without looking up at me.

"Please," I said.

That got him to look up. "What did you say?" he asked.

My heart started pounding *thumpa-thumpa-thumpa* in my ears. "I just asked for cookies for the kids."

"What did you say after that?"

I took a step backward. "Uh, I said *please*." How could he have confused that with something obscene? The only word I could think of that sounded anything like it was "peas." Did that somehow have a meaning I didn't know about? "Never mind," I said.

"Hang on, hang on," he muttered. He reached under the counter, pulled out a brown paper lunch bag and put four chocolate chip cookies inside. Then he held out the bag.

For a second, I just stared at him with *stupid* written all over my face. Then I took the cookies. "Thank you," I said.

He nodded. "You're welcome. You've got nice manners."

The mom and the kids were waiting for me by the end of the table. I swung my backpack up onto my shoulder and walked over to them. I handed her the bag. "For later," I said.

Her hand reached out toward me. She hesitated, and then she went with her first impulse and touched my arm. "Thank you for everything today," she said.

"Thank you for letting me eat lunch with you," I said.

We walked outside together. Dylan pulled at my jacket before I could leave. "What's your name?" he asked.

He was way too serious for a kid who wasn't much more than maybe six.

"My name is Maddie," I said.

"Mine's Dylan, if you forgot," he said.

The lump in my throat came back, and I had to swallow it away before I could answer. "I remember," I told him.

Halfway to the street, I turned back for a look at them. When Dylan did the same, I waved and he waved back. I didn't turn around again.

Q pulled up at the library just a couple of minutes after six. I was happy to see the white Honda coming down the street. My back and shoulders were starting to ache from carrying the bag of clean stuff around.

We drove over to the hotel, and Q found a place to park on the street about a block and a half away. I stayed in the car while he went for the food. The smell of spices and garlic filled the car as we drove up the hill.

We followed the same routine as the night before. I drove the car into the garage bay, and then we walked around checking all the doors. There was nothing left in the kitchen but the stove, but at least it was still working. Supper was some kind of salad with tiny tomatoes, tiny slices of spicy beef and fancy lettuce.

"What's wrong with this?" I asked Q. We were sitting on my sofa with our feet propped on the desk.

"Who knows," he said around a mouthful of lettuce. "I'm guessing the meat. It was probably too rare. Or not rare enough."

"I don't get how people can be so picky about their food," I said.

Q reached over and turned the crank on the radio a few times. "If I left anything on my plate, even just one bite of food, my old man would go into this rant about all the starving children in the world who would be happy to have it."

He was wearing his knit hat again, and his hair was sticking out at weird angles. It was kind of cute.

"That's not the same thing," I said.

He put his plastic fork down and leaned his head against the back of the couch. The band on the radio was singing about taking care of business. "One time I told him I'd mail what was left on my plate to those hungry kids." He laughed, but there wasn't really anything funny in the sound. "I didn't do that twice."

I didn't know what to say. I bumped his arm with my shoulder. "What's for dessert?" I asked.

"Good question." He put his plate on the desk and reached over me for the takeout bag. He looked inside the Styrofoam clamshell and then wiggled his eyebrows at me. It looked like he was having some sort of spasm, and I burst out laughing.

"Hey, chocolate cheesecake is serious business," he said.

"Chocolate cheesecake?" I leaned forward for a better look.

"Eat your vegetables," he said with pretend seriousness. "Remember all those starving kids."

I thought about Dylan then. I hoped he had something for supper. I hoped they all did.

Q dropped down beside me. "Maddie, you okay?"

I speared a tomato with my fork and then set it back down again. "When I went to Pax to put the laundry in a locker, I saw this mother with three little kids—one was just a baby." I sighed. "I wish I could feed all the hungry children in the world."

"You said you wanted to go to school someday," Q said. "What do you want to be?"

I picked up my fork again. "You'll laugh," I said.

He shook his head slowly. "No, I won't. Tell me." When I didn't answer right away, he bumped me with his shoulder. "C'mon Maddie, what?"

"A doctor," I said softly.

"Wow!" Q said.

"Stupid, right?"

He set the takeout container on the sofa beside him. "No. I could see you as a doctor."

I looked at him. "Yeah, right," I said.

He pulled off his hat and ran both hands back through his hair so it stuck out all over his head. "I'm serious," he said. "You're smart, or you wouldn't have made it on your own. And I've seen how kind you are. So yeah, you could be a doctor."

It was the first time someone hadn't laughed when I said I wanted to be a doctor—not that I said it very often. It felt good and weird all at the same time.

"What about you, Q?" I said, mostly to change the subject. "Is there anything else you want to do besides have a farm? Maybe get a business degree, or go to law school?"

Q snorted with laughter. "Me in school? Uh-uh. Too much reading, too much talking about doing stuff instead of just going and doing it." He traced a seam along the bottom edge of the couch. "I get that if you want to be a doctor you have to go to school, but it's just not my thing."

Abruptly he stood up. "You ready for cheesecake?" he asked.

I pulled the tomato off my fork, popped it into my mouth and nodded. I'd noticed that when Q didn't want to talk about something, he changed the subject or made a joke. That was fine with me. There was stuff I didn't like talking about either.

We spent the next two nights at the building. Each morning, Q drove me downtown. Then I walked through the park and along the riverbank trail picking up returnable bottles. I made four trips to the recycling center and ended up with just over thirty dollars. Lucky for me, people were pigs. I divided the money the way I always did: a third for day-to-day necessities, a third for my emergency fund and the rest for my education fund.

I hadn't told Hannah—I hadn't told anyone—but I was going back to school, just as soon as I had enough money to rent a room. I figured I could get by without a phone, but I did need an address to get an education.

Afternoons, I kept on at my math at the library. When I did get to school, I didn't plan on being the stupidest person in the class.

five

Saturday night we went back to the parking lot at All-mart. Q's friend wasn't working, so we'd decided to buy a pizza. He walked over to Pizza Man hoping to score one that didn't get picked up for half the price it was supposed to be. I was heading back to the car from the washroom, cutting between the lines of cars, when I heard a little voice call my name. I looked around, trying to follow the sound. At the end of the line of campers was a beat-up dark-blue van. A little blond kid was standing beside it waving. Dylan. "Maddie," he called again.

I waved so he'd know I'd seen him, gesturing that he should stay there. "Hi, Dylan," I said when I got over to him. I looked around for the rest of the family. "Where's your mom?"

"I'm supposed to say she's in there." He pointed at the mall.

Supposed to? The hairs started prickling on the back of my neck. I scrunched down to his level. "Where is she really? You can tell me."

He chewed on his bottom lip. What was I supposed to do? Just leave him by himself the way it seemed his mom had? I smiled and fought the urge to throw my arms around him, which probably would have scared the crap out of him.

He shifted from one foot to the other. "She took Summer to get her owie fixed," he finally said.

Okay, which one was Summer? The baby or the toddler?

Dylan's big blue eyes looked up at me shyly. "I'm baby-sitting Luke," he said.

I could feel my heartbeat thumping in both ears. "Where is Luke?" I asked.

He pointed at the van. I stood up and squinted through the windshield. The passenger seat had been tipped backward, and a small person was curled up in it, covered with a jacket. It was the toddler, not the baby.

I leaned against the fender of the van. The only thing I could think about was all the weirdos in the world. They weren't all standing on the table reciting Shakespeare. In fact, I was pretty sure that guy was harmless. The real weirdos walked around looking like all the rest of us. How easy would it be to grab Dylan and his little brother? The fact that I was standing here with him showed how little effort it would take.

I tucked a stray strand of hair behind my ear. Okay, what the heck should I do? Tell Dylan to get in the van and stay there till his mother came back? Take both kids to the Honda?

Dylan reached over and slid his hand into mine. It struck me that to him, I was a grown-up who could fix everything. Right. I was sleeping in a car and keeping my money in the bottom of my shoe.

His little hand was warm in mine. "Dylan, what kind of an owie did Summer have?" I asked.

"I dunno," he said.

"Did she fall?"

He shook his head. "No. But she cried a lot last night and she kept pulling at her ear. Do you think her ear is broken?"

I shook my head. "No. I think she just needs some medicine to make her feel better." It was Saturday night. Dylan's mom had probably taken the baby to the emergency room. It could be hours before she came back. Why hadn't she taken the other two kids with her?

"Dylan, how come you stayed here?" I asked.

He made a face and looked at me like I was stupid. "I told you, I'm babysitting Luke," he said hotly.

"I know," I said.

"And Daddy is bringing supper. Do you think he'll be here soon? I'm hungry."

Daddy? I'd figured Dylan's mom was all by herself with the kids. There was a dad? So where the heck was he?

"Was Daddy here when your mom took Summer to get her owie fixed?"

He kicked a rock under the van and bent to see where it went.

"Dylan," I said.

"Daddy was supposed to be the babysitter, but he said I'm a big boy and I could do it." His voice was muffled against the front of his jacket.

I blew out a breath. Even at her worst, my mother had never left me by myself. I looked around uncertainly. Dylan was on his hands and knees, peering under the old van. Then I spotted Q. He had just crossed the street and was coming up the grass to the parking lot. He was carrying a cardboard pizza box. I stepped out away from the van and waited for him to look in my direction. When he did, I waved, and he changed direction.

"Stay there," I said to Dylan. I took a few steps forward to meet Q.

He looked from me to the van and back again. "What are you doing?" he asked.

"Remember I told you about meeting that mom and her kids a few days ago?"

He nodded slowly.

I could smell the pizza, and my stomach rumbled with hunger. "Well, two of the kids are here."

Dylan had gotten up and was standing by the front wheel of the van, watching us.

"Where's their mother?" Q asked.

"I'm guessing the emergency room. It sounds like the baby has an ear infection."

Q put a hand on top of his head. "And she left two kids here."

I crossed my arms over my chest. "As far as I can figure out, the dad left them here by themselves." I tipped my head toward Dylan. "That's Dylan. His little brother is asleep in the van. He says his dad went to get supper and left him 'babysitting.'"

Q's mouth pulled into a thin, tight line. "Shit," he muttered.

"What do I do?" I asked. "I can't leave them here."

"It's okay," Q said. "You said the kid's name is Dylan?"

I nodded.

He leaned around me and smiled at the little boy. "Hi, Dylan. I'm Maddie's friend, Q."

"Q isn't a name," Dylan said. "It's a letter. Q, R, S, T, U, V."

"You're right," Q said. "But it can be a name too. You know, I knew somebody once whose name was Seven."

Dylan scrunched up his nose. "That's just silly," he said.

Q nodded. "That's what I thought."

"Is that pizza?" Dylan asked.

"Uh-huh," Q said. "You hungry?"

"I'm not supposed to take stuff from people I don't know."

Right. Teach the kid not to take stuff from people he doesn't know, and then go leave him in the parking lot at the mall. There was good parenting.

"That's a really good rule," Q said. "So I'm going to get Maddie to give you a piece of pizza, because you know her."

That seemed to make sense to Dylan. Q pulled some napkins out of his pocket, and I opened the pizza box and pulled out a slice, setting it on a couple of the paper napkins. I handed it to Dylan. "Be careful," I warned him. "It's hot."

He nodded. "Thank you," he said.

I watched him take a careful bite from the end and, for a second, I almost burst into tears.

Q fished a small bottle of water out of his other pocket and handed it to me. I unscrewed the top and gave Dylan a drink. Again he thanked me.

I leaned over to check on his little brother in the front seat. He was still asleep. My stomach made another loud rumble.

"Have something to eat, Maddie," Q said softly. "It doesn't do the kid or anyone else any good for you to go hungry."

He handed me a couple of napkins and I pulled apart two slices, one for myself and one for him. I squatted down next to Dylan and ate mine. Q put the pizza box on the hood of the van and leaned against the side to eat his.

I was wiping sauce of Dylan's face when his father came back. "Hey!" he shouted. "What the hell are you doing with my van?"

Not *What are you doing with my kid?*, but *What are you doing with my van?* I felt my chest tighten, and at the same time I put an arm around Dylan, who was looking wide-eyed and scared in his father's direction.

Q pushed himself upright. "Stay here," he said quietly. He stepped forward to intercept Dylan's dad, standing with his feet apart and his hands in his pockets.

"What the fuck do you think you're doing?" the man said. He made a move to get around Q, who stepped in front of him and put out his hand.

I couldn't hear what Q was saying, but even from the back, I could see the tension in his body. He was maybe a bit taller than Dylan's dad, and I got the sense if it came to a fight, Q would win. Now there was a good idea, them getting into a fight while Dylan watched.

"My dad's mad," Dylan said softly.

I gave his shoulders a squeeze. "I think he was just worried about you and your brother."

He shook his head and stared at his feet. "No, it's my fault. I was supposed to stay in the van."

I didn't know what to say, so I gave him another squeeze.

In a minute or so, Q turned around and he and Dylan's dad walked over to us. "Maddie," Q said. "This is Michael."

"Hi," I said. Michael was a bit heavier than Q, with short dirty-blond hair and a couple of days' stubble. He had the same blue-gray eyes as Dylan, but there was a mean glint to Michael's gaze. Or maybe I just thought that because I already didn't like him. I kept my arm around Dylan. I'd decided if his father did anything mean, I was going to scoop the kid up and run like hell.

Michael looked at Dylan. "Is your brother still sleeping?" Dylan nodded. Michael shot Q a quick sideways glance, no more than a flick of his eyes. I probably wouldn't have seen it if I hadn't been watching his face so closely. Michael leaned toward Dylan, who leaned back against me just a little. "You did good," he said.

"I did?" Dylan looked up at me for confirmation, and I nodded slightly.

I noticed then that Michael was carrying fast food. At the same time it was registering that it shouldn't have taken so long for him to go get some greasy hamburgers, I realized I could smell alcohol on the man. He'd been somewhere for a drink. Or two. He was a crappy father cliché.

Michael handed the bag to Dylan. "Here," he said. "Wake your brother up and give him something to eat."

Dylan took the food, at the same time reaching for my hand and squeezing it. I squeezed back, then opened the door and helped him climb into the driver's seat of the van.

"See you, Maddie," he whispered.

"See you," I whispered back.

I turned around to find Michael watching me and Q watching him.

"You know my wife," Michael said. He didn't look like he smiled much.

"A little," I said.

"Man, I'm sorry about the misunderstanding," Q said. "It's just, Maddie loves kids."

"Shit, you want one?" Michael asked. "You can't get a break, you know?" He wiped a hand across his face. "First I lose my job, and then the kids need so goddamn much crap, you know? You have any idea what diapers and all that shit cost?"

"Lucky for me, I don't," Q said.

What the heck was he talking about? I shot him a glare, but his expression didn't change.

I saw Q look to see if the kids were okay in the van. "We gotta get going," he said to Michael. "You need a baby-sitter, like I said, Maddie loves kids." He reached for my hand. I grabbed the pizza box, thinking I was going to beat the crap out of Q with it the first chance I got.

"And sorry about before," Q added.

Michael shrugged. "Not a problem."

Q and I walked away, and I waited until we were out of sight of the van before I stopped and let go of his hand. "What was all that crap?" I said. "That guy's a jerk."

"I know," Q said evenly.

I glared at him. One of my hands was clenched in my pocket. The other was crushing the pizza box. "You know? So what was all that 'Maddie loves kids' and 'Sorry about before'?"

Q started walking again, and I had to scramble after him. "Maddie, if I get into a pissing contest with that guy, who do you think's gonna pay for it?"

I had to take a bunch of deep breaths before I could say anything. "You think he'd…" I couldn't finish the sentence.

"I know he would," Q said. "Better he thinks he got the better of me than he thinks he looked like a fool."

I looked back over my shoulder. "We can't leave them with him."

Q caught my arm. "Yes, we can. He's their father."

I tried to pull away, but Q held on to me. "He left two little kids by themselves. And don't say you didn't smell him, Q."

"Let it be, Maddie," Q said. "I know Michael was drinking. I know everything someone like Michael does. Believe me. But he's their dad, and you're just a kid living on the street. Who do you think anyone's gonna believe?"

I finally yanked my arm out of Q's grip, but I didn't bolt back to the van. "So I'm just supposed to do nothing?" I blinked a couple of times because all of a sudden there was something in my eye.

"No. We're going to be here for a few days, and so are they. You heard me tell him you could babysit."

"Yeah."

"So maybe you'll get the chance. And maybe you'll be able to find out how Michael treats the kids."

I looked at him then. He was rubbing a hand up and down his arm. "Look, Maddie, I don't want to see those kids with a dad who…" He shook his head and didn't finish. "But taking them away and putting them in foster care? That's sending them to hell."

I turned away, scraping my shoe on the ground.

"Let's go back to the car," Q said.

We walked the rest of the way to the Honda, which was parked about three quarters of the way down the row of trailers, tucked in between a big RV and a much smaller Volkswagen van. I got in the passenger side, leaned my head back against the headrest and closed my eyes. Q took the pizza box out of my hands and set it on the dashboard.

"I hate not being able to do anything," I said.

"So someday you'll become a doctor, and you *will* be able to do something."

"That's too far away."

I could hear Q moving in the driver's seat, probably trying to get his long legs into a comfortable position. "Dylan knows he can trust you," he said finally. "That's something."

I thought about all the adults in my life. My mother. The guidance counselor who'd shaken her head when I'd said I wanted to be a doctor. Evan. Maybe Q was right. Maybe Dylan's knowing he could count on me was something. I opened my eyes.

Q was sitting cross-legged on the seat watching me. "You all right?" he asked.

I nodded.

He gave the pizza box a poke. "You want a slice? It's cold and probably stuck to the cardboard. Yummy!" He did the spazzy eyebrow thing.

That made me laugh, even though I didn't feel like it. "Okay," I said.

Q opened the mashed-in lid of the box and got a piece of pizza for each of us. The cheese was chewy, kind of like a pencil eraser, and the crust was soggy. "Yummy," I said to Q, mimicking his eyebrow thing. That got me a smile.

After we ate, Q collected the garbage. "You're a good person too, Q," I said quietly.

He stopped but didn't say anything, I reached out and caught his hand. He gave it a quick squeeze, the way I'd done with Dylan, and then he got out of the car.

Six

When I woke up, I could hear Q moving in the backseat.

"Hey, I'm sorry," he said. "Did I wake you up?"

I pushed my hair back out of my eyes and sat up. "Nah, my arm's all weird." I stuck out my right arm, rolling it from the shoulder until it made a loud snap.

Q shuddered.

One of my blankets had slipped to the floor. I opened the car door and got out, stretching my arms over my head. Q climbed out of the backseat. "If you make that noise again, I'll puke," he warned.

"You're such a wussy boy," I teased.

"I'm not a wussy boy," he said. "With those shoulders, you should be in a freak show."

"How do you know I wasn't?"

He laughed. "You win. I got nothing." Then his face got serious. "We'll have to go to Tim's to get cleaned up. They don't open the mall until eleven."

"I'll buy you a breakfast sandwich," I said. He started to object, but I held up a hand. "It's my bottle money, and besides, you got the pizza last night."

I put my hair back in a braid, pulled on my jacket and dug the sleep crud out of my eyes. Q locked the car and we started for Tim's. I couldn't help looking down the row of RVs for the old blue van. There was no activity around it.

"He's okay," Q said.

I nodded and hoped he was right.

It was quiet at Tim's. I got washed up, changing into my second-to-last clean shirt. Then Q and I sat at a table by the window and had our coffee and sandwiches.

"Hey, Maddie, I got something I gotta do this morning," he said.

"Did that guy lend you his truck?" I asked.

Q pulled a piece of bacon out of his sandwich and ate it. "No. All that stuff ended up going to the dump. What a waste." He stretched his legs under the table. "It's that I kinda promised I'd do something this morning."

"Okay," I said.

"There's this woman…she's old and she doesn't have much, plus she's raising her granddaughter, I met them at the food bank a couple of times. She needs a couple of screens put on her windows, but the landlord keeps putting her off. I told her I'd do it."

He looked kind of embarrassed, pushing his coffee cup back and forth across the table from one hand to the other.

"That's really nice of you," I said.

"It's not a problem," he said. "And I like her." He looked up at me then. "So is there anywhere I could take you?"

It was my turn to look down, embarrassed. "You'll laugh," I said.

"No, I won't."

"Church."

"Church?"

I looked up at him and nodded.

"Okay, you have clearly been taken over by the Holy Roller pod people," Q said.

"See?" I said. "I knew you'd laugh."

Q pushed his cup away. "I'm not laughing. I'm just trying to figure out why the heck you want to go to church. Didn't you get enough 'Come to Jesus' on Monday night?"

Had it just been Monday night that I'd met Q? I'd only known him a week, but it felt a lot longer. "It's not like that," I said. "There's this big old church down by the river."

He nodded. "I know the place. With the copper roof?"

"Yeah. Sometimes I like to go there. I can just sit in the back and listen to the music, and no one bothers me. I like it. It's peaceful."

They had a couple of services on Sunday morning, and sometimes I'd sit through both of them, putting a dollar in the collection plate each time. I didn't mind. I figured it was a pretty good deal to be out of the weather and wrapped in all the music.

And no one ever bothered me. I noticed a lot of students, and I just managed to blend in with them. A couple of times, I'd even gone for cookies and coffee in the hall after the service, walking around with my cup, smiling like I belonged.

"Okay, so I'll drive you down," Q said.

We finished eating, and I brushed my teeth in the bathroom. Then Q and I walked back to the car. Most of the RV people were up and moving around. It was still quiet at Dylan's family's van.

"Do you think the baby is okay?" I asked Q.

"Yeah," he said, eyeing the van himself. "Little kids get sick all the time, and they're better before you know it."

I nodded, but I couldn't stop myself from watching for some sign that Dylan and his brother and sister were okay.

It was still early when Q left me at the church, so I crossed the street and walked along the river for a while. When I did go in and find a seat, I found myself staring at the huge cross at the front. I looked around to see if anyone was watching, then I bent my head and closed my eyes. *Thank you for Q and for having food and somewhere to sleep*, I prayed silently. *Please watch out for Dylan and his brother and sister. Amen.*

I felt a little silly when I opened my eyes again, but if you couldn't pray in a church, then where could you do it? I hoped God was listening. I'd been in the church enough to know that here they believed that God was always listening, and I hoped for Dylan's sake that he was.

When I came out about quarter after twelve, Q was across the street sitting on the hood of the Honda in the sun. It felt good to have someone waiting for me, to not have to walk around the city for hours and then scramble to get something to eat and find somewhere to sleep. That cramped little car was starting to feel like home.

"How was church?" Q asked, pushing his sunglasses up onto his head.

"Nice," I said. "They did something called a cantata. The music was beautiful."

He slid down off the car.

"How was your friend?"

Q shook his head. "I thought she seemed tired. She said she wasn't, but that's just how she is." He reached for the car door handle. "I gotta get gas, so that means either the soup line or Pax for lunch."

I got in the passenger side. It would be hard to avoid Hannah if we went to Pax. If we went to the Community Kitchen, there was a chance I'd see Dylan and his family. And I'd have Q with me.

"Soup line?" I asked.

He grinned and pulled his shades back down. "Your wish is my command."

We parked the car a couple of blocks away from the Community Kitchen. Leaving it any closer was just asking for it to be trashed while we were in there. The line was long, and there was already some pushing and loud voices at the front. Q stood close behind me, and just the sense of him there, even though we weren't touching, made me feel safer. I scanned the line for Dylan or his mother, or even Michael, but I didn't see them.

It was soup day—chicken vegetable with lots of veggies. Q and I took our bowls and a roll each and went to sit at the same table I'd sat at with Dylan's mother and the children. I looked around the room. They weren't there.

"They might have gone to Pax," Q said.

That made sense. I was dipping the last bit of my roll in my soup when he touched my arm. "Maddie," he said. He pointed to the door. Michael was just joining the end of the line. His wife was behind, shepherding the children forward. She looked worn-out. Dylan looked scared, cowed, but he was holding his little brother's hand.

I moved to get up to go over to them, but Q put out a hand to stop me. "Don't," he said.

"Why? I just want to make sure the kids are okay."

"You'll piss off their father."

I would have pulled my hand away, but I couldn't. "Just by saying hello?"

Q scooped up a spoonful of vegetables and let them fall back into his bowl. "Yes. Just by saying hello. Stay here. Let them come to you. I know what I'm taking about. Just pick up your spoon and eat. Please, Maddie."

I swallowed. I picked up my spoon and pretended to eat while I watched the family work their way through the line. Q let go of my other arm.

They took a table about halfway from the back on the end wall. Michael started eating right away while his wife helped the two boys get settled. I wanted to go over and help her. No, that's not true. I wanted to go over and dump that bowl of soup on Michael's head.

I realized Q was watching them too when he said softly, "He's an asshole."

Dylan's mother shifted the baby from one arm to the other, and even out of the corner of my eye, I knew she'd spotted us by the way her body language changed. She bent and kissed the top of Dylan's head, and I had to put my spoon down again, because there was no way anything was getting past the lump in my throat.

At least Dylan had her, I reminded myself, and it was clear that she loved him. I turned my head for just a quick look at him. He was eating and talking to his mother.

"Don't stare at them," Q said. "Look at me, Maddie. Talk to me."

"This is not a place for little kids," I said through clenched teeth.

"I know," Q said. He put down his spoon and ran his palm across his chin and down his neck. He hadn't shaved for a couple of days. The dark stubble made him look older, and then I realized with a shock that I didn't actually know how old he was.

"Maddie, Michael is the kind of guy who always has to prove he has the biggest set of balls in the room. Anything or anybody that challenges that, means he'll strike out. The thing is, he'll strike out at her and those kids."

I played with the zipper on my jacket. "So you want me to just pretend I don't see what a dip wad he is."

He blew out a breath. "For now, yeah. Like I told you last night, no one's going to listen to us."

It didn't feel like anyone had heard my prayer after all. I made myself eat the rest of the soup. I didn't look directly over at Dylan and his family, but I did sneak little sideways glances. I was pretty sure Q noticed, but he pretended he didn't.

"We should go, Maddie," he said finally. He stood up and took our dishes back to the counter. I swung around and sat with my back to Michael and his family, because otherwise I knew I'd stare at them, or even worse, go over and make a mess of things. So I didn't see Michael get up and come toward us as Q came back to the table.

"Hey, guys," Michael said.

"Hey," Q said. He stood in front of me in the same position as he had taken last night, hands in his pockets, feet apart.

"You got any plans for this afternoon?" Michael asked. I noticed the jacket he was wearing was a lot nicer than the ones the kids had. And his blond hair looked like it had been cut fairly recently by someone who knew what they were doing with a pair of scissors.

Q shrugged. Michael looked at me. My heart was suddenly pounding.

"You said you like kids. Could you watch Dylan for a while? We gotta take the baby back to the doctor, and I think the other one has something too." He rolled his eyes. "Kids. They get every freakin' germ out there."

I knew I had to play this right. I looked up at Q. "Would it be okay?" I asked.

He nodded and then turned to Michael. "Yeah, she'll watch the kid for you."

Michael gave me a lazy smile. "You goin' back up to the mall?"

Q nodded.

"Okay, man, I'll see you up there in about half an hour."

"Yeah, that's good," Q said.

Michael walked back to his family. "C'mon," Q said.

I followed him out. "That was good," he said as we headed for the car.

"I figured if he thought I didn't have a brain of my own, it might be a good thing," I said. I didn't know what to do with my hands. I suddenly had the urge to punch something. Or someone.

"I'm sorry," Q said.

I stopped walking. "What are you sorry for?"

"We should just tell that jerk to go shove it." He made a fist with one hand and smacked his other palm with it.

"Yeah, and she and the kids'll pay for it," I said. "You're right. Nobody is going to listen to us. A couple of runaways against a husband and father." I remembered how my mother's face got closed when I told her that Evan had hit me. No, no, he was a good Christian. He wouldn't have done something like that. I was lying. I was making it up.

"Anyway, we get Dylan for the afternoon," I said. "That's good, right?"

Q looked at me and smiled. "Yes, it is," he said.

He looked ahead to where the car was and then back at me. "I'll race you," he said. "One, two…"

I didn't wait for three. I was off like a shot, tearing down the sidewalk. Q came flying up behind me, passing me easily. He leaned against the car to catch his breath.

"No fair," I gasped. "Your legs are longer than mine. They're mutant legs, alien legs."

"Hey, you cheated," he said, pulling a hand through his hair. "You're supposed to wait until I say three."

I reached for the door handle on my side. "You didn't say that."

"It's understood."

"Not by me."

His fixed his dark eyes on my face. "Cheater."

"Alien legs."

We glared at each other, and then we both started laughing at the same time. And suddenly I felt good. The sun was shining, and at least for this afternoon, I'd know Dylan was okay.

It was more like forty-five minutes before Michael showed up with Dylan in tow. We'd pulled the Honda back into the same parking spot between the RV and the van. I was starting to get crazy, thinking maybe Michael wasn't going to show after all. He came down the line of trailers with Dylan behind him. He didn't hold the kid's hand. He didn't even look back once to see if he was there. Dylan had a plastic grocery bag in one hand. He stood quietly behind his father. "I figure we'll be two, three hours at the most," Michael said.

"Sure," Q said. He inclined his head in my direction. "They'll be fine."

"Great," Michael said. He looked down at Dylan. "Hey, you be good."

Dylan nodded his head slowly. "I will," he said.

"Okay, see ya," Michael said, and he was gone.

I smiled at Dylan. "What's in the bag?" I asked.

He looked down at the Superstore bag. "That's Fred," he said. "He doesn't like always having to stay in the van and be quiet."

"Me neither," Q said behind me. "I like making noise." He started dancing from one foot to the other, waving his arms above his head and singing, "Oooh laa, rah, rah, rah!"

"What is that?" I asked.

"It's the bird dance," Q said.

I made a face at Dylan. "We can do a better bird dance than that, can't we?"

I twisted at the waist, tucked my hands in my armpits, and flapped my elbows like wings. I must have looked like a total spazoid, but it was worth it to see Dylan begin to smile and start his own arm-flapping dance.

Q stopped first and dropped, panting, into a squat. I sagged against the front fender of the car. Dylan hopped around for about a minute longer. Then he stopped and looked up at me. I leaned forward. "What is it?" I asked.

"Fred has to pee," he whispered.

It was after twelve, so the mall was open. "Let's take him in to the bathroom," I said, offering my hand.

Dylan wouldn't take it. "Fred doesn't like to pee in the girls' room," he said.

I looked over my shoulder at Q.

"Of course he doesn't," Q said. "We're men. We don't pee with girls. We pee with guys." He got to his feet. "C'mon. We'll take Fred to the men's room."

Dylan put his hand in mine then, and we walked across the parking lot to the mall washroom. I looked down the row of campers. The old blue van was gone.

Fred turned out to be a small brown teddy bear in a red jacket. Q took Dylan and the bear into the men's room, and I made a quick dash to the women's washroom.

Just like I never turned down food, I never missed a chance to pee.

"I washed my hands," Dylan said when he came out.

"Me too," Q said, holding out both of his hands, palms up.

"Good job," I said. We headed for the door. "What do you want to do?" I asked Dylan.

"I don't know," he said.

I looked back at Q, who was behind us. "Could we go to the park?" I whispered.

He nodded.

"Wanna go to the park?" I said to Dylan.

"I don't have to stay in your car?" Dylan asked.

"No," I said. "We can swing. We can climb the monkey bars."

"Fred likes the swings," he said.

I leaned down toward the grocery bag. "Hey, Fred," I stage-whispered. "Wanna go to the park?" Then I frowned and tipped my head to one side. "What was that?" I asked. I waited, and then I smiled at Dylan. "He said yes."

We drove down to the park that was halfway between Pax House and the Community Kitchen. I pushed Dylan and Fred the bear on the swings until my shoulders ached.

"Higher, Maddie," Dylan urged. "Higher!" A faint whisper of memory, of me, swings and my dad floated through my mind. I felt that ache of missing him I sometimes got. I knew it wasn't really missing him; it was missing the idea of him, because you can't miss what you can't remember very well.

It took some time, but we even got Fred to try the slide. He was way too scared to go down by himself, so Fred sat on Dylan's lap and Dylan sat on my lap. Then Fred decided to give the monkey bars a go. That was Q's department.

He helped the small brown bear climb up and sit on a rung about two thirds of the way from the top. Then Dylan decided he had to try it.

I stood by the bars, which were shaped sort of like a red metal igloo and watched Dylan climb while I bit the inside of my cheek. I was way more scared of the monkey bars than Fred the bear was, but I didn't want Dylan or Q to know that.

When Dylan, Fred and Q were back on the ground, Q said it was time to head back up the hill. Dylan didn't argue. He tucked the bear back into the plastic bag and took my hand.

It was quarter to four, and there was no sign of the blue van. We parked at the top end of the row, next to a dark-brown RV that was as big as a bus. We walked down the row of travel trailers and back up again. Nothing. I looked at Q over the top of Dylan's blond head.

"They could have gotten held up," Q said softly. "And he's the type to take advantage. It's okay."

We took Dylan in for another pee. I had a granola bar in my backpack, and I gave him half.

"We'll go down the mall," I told Q.

"Okay," he said. "I'll go back to the car and watch for them."

I walked Dylan down the mall. We stopped at every kiddie ride so he could get on. I didn't have any money to make them shake or bounce up and down, but Dylan didn't care. He made *vroom-vroom* sounds in the red race car and said *giddyup* to the purple horse. He was too busy making all the sticks and buttons move in the black helicopter to do any sound effects. When he got on the giraffe, Fred insisted that I ride the elephant. I kind of felt like a dork, especially when a couple of girls about my age walked by and laughed. Then I reminded myself they could have been laughing about my clothes or my hair or maybe not even about me at all.

Q was sitting on the hood of the car when we came out of the mall. He shook his head slightly as we walked over to him. "Is my mom here?" Dylan asked.

"Not yet," Q said. "She's probably still at the doctor."

I squatted down to his level. "Are you tired?" I asked.

He shook his head. "No, but Fred is."

"So how about Fred gets in the backseat and has a nap, and you keep him company?"

"Okay," Dylan said. "Fred still takes naps because he's younger than me. I don't take naps because I'm a big boy."

I settled him in the backseat with one of my blankets and then went to sit next to Q. "Where are they?" I said.

"I don't know," he said, pushing his sunglasses up on his head. "I've been around this end of the lot three times."

"They are coming back for him, aren't they?"

Q blew out a breath and tilted his head to one side to look at me.

"Aren't they?" I repeated.

"I don't know," he said finally.

I looked over my shoulder, through the windshield. Dylan was asleep, his head against the back of the car seat, hugging the bag with the teddy bear inside to his chest.

I pressed a hand to my own chest and closed my eyes for a few moments. When I opened them, Q was watching me. "What do we do?" I asked.

"They'll probably be back," Q said, but he didn't sound convinced.

"What if they're not?"

He shook his head. "Don't go there for now," he said.

seven

They didn't come at five o'clock. At five thirty, I gave Q some of my money for supper. When he came back, I woke up Dylan and sat with him while he ate chicken nuggets and yogurt.

"Maddie, where's my mom?" he asked. "Is she still at the doctor?"

"I don't know," I said. "Sometimes doctors can be real slow."

Q was sitting in the front seat. He pointed to the parking lot and got out. I wiped a blob of yogurt from Dylan's chin. "Share with Fred," I told him.

"Where are you going?" he asked, one hand reaching for me.

"I'm just going to talk to Q," I said. "You can see me through the window. I promise." I got out and then turned around and waved at Dylan. "He's scared," I said to Q. I folded my arms across my chest. "What do we do? Do we go to the police?"

Q shook his head. "No." He zipped his jacket. "I'm going to go down to the hospital. It's possible the other two are really sick and they're still there."

"We'll come with you?"

"No. I don't want to scare the kid."

I looked back at Dylan again and made myself smile at him through the side window. "Take the car, then," I told Q. "We'll be okay here for a while, or I can take him over to Tim's."

"He's better where he is," Q said. "It's not that far, and maybe I can even hitch."

I sighed. "All right, but be careful. Don't get in with any weirdos."

He leaned over and tucked a loose strand of hair behind my ear. "I'll be as fast as I can," he said. He fished in his jacket pocket and pulled out the keys to the car. "Here," he said. "In case you have to take him to the bathroom or something. Lock the car."

"I will," I said, tucking the key ring in the pocket of my jeans. I watched him head out, cutting rapidly across the lot. I felt for the shard of glass in my jacket pocket. It wasn't a knife, but it would do. Then I got back in with Dylan.

"Where is Q going?" he asked.

"He's going to see if he can find your mom and dad," I said.

"Maybe they got lost."

"Maybe they did."

I ate the last couple of chicken nuggets and finished his milk. Then I wiped his face with a paper napkin, and we walked the trash over to one of the garbage cans next to a cart corral.

"What do you want to do, kiddo?" I asked.

"Sometimes my mom sings us songs," he said.

"I'm not a very good singer."

His face fell.

"How about 'Twinkle, Twinkle Little Bat'?"

He frowned. "That's not a song. It's 'Twinkle Twinkle Little Star.'"

"It is too a song," I said. Then I sang softly, "Twinkle, twinkle, little bat! How I wonder what you're at! Up above the world you fly, like a tea tray in the sky. Twinkle, twinkle, little bat! How I wonder what you're at!"

He laughed. "Maddie, that's silly. You made it up."

I shook my head. "No I didn't. It's from a book called *Alice in Wonderland*."

He leaned against me. "What's the book about?"

I put my arm around him. "It's about a girl named Alice and all the things that happen to her."

"Are there any trains in the book?" he asked. "I like books about trains."

"I don't think there are any trains in *Alice in Wonderland*," I said. "There's a cat, and a rabbit."

He yawned. "I wish I could have a cat," he said. "But my mom said it wouldn't be fair to make it stay in our van all the time."

He snuggled in next to me. "I think your mom's right," I said. I leaned left a little to see if there was any sign of Q, but I didn't see him.

"Maddie, am I going to have a sleepover with you?" Dylan asked. He reached for the grocery bag with his bear and pulled it closer.

"Maybe," I said.

"That's what I thought," he said.

It felt as though cold fingers were crawling their way up my back. "What do you mean, Dylan?" I asked.

He laughed. "I wouldn't have my pajamas and tooth-brush if we weren't going to have a sleepover."

I looked down at the bag he was still hanging on to. They weren't coming back for him. Not tonight, for sure. Maybe not ever.

"You know what?" I said. "We need to go brush your teeth and pee before bed." I was surprised at how normal my voice sounded.

"Can we wait for Q?" he asked. "I don't want to pee in the girls' room."

"Sorry, kiddo," I said. "You have to use the girls' bath-room this time."

He made a face at me.

"And it's all pinky and lacy in there."

"Is not!" he said hotly.

I forced a big smile that my face didn't feel like making. "Oh yes it is," I said. "You'll see."

I helped Dylan do up his jacket, got my backpack and made sure he was still holding on to the plastic bag. It was going to have to be Tim's. The mall was dark and locked. "Tell you what," I said. "You walk for part of the way, and I'll carry you some."

I swung my backpack onto my shoulder just as the side door to the RV beside us opened. "I'm sorry," the woman coming out and I said at the same time. I took a step back so she could step down.

She noticed Dylan and smiled at him. She was the gray-haired grandmotherly type.

He held up his bag. "We're going to brush my teeth."

"Good for you," she said.

Dylan scrunched up his nose. "Maddie says I have to go in the girls' bathroom. I don't like the girls' bathroom. She says it's pink, but I think she made that part up."

I felt my face getting red. I held out my hand to Dylan. "C'mon," I said. "We'd better go."

The gray-haired woman gestured at her trailer. "Would you like to use my bathroom?" she asked.

"Is it pink?" Dylan asked.

"Dylan!" I shook my head at him.

"No, it's not pink," she said to Dylan. "It's white and blue." She looked at me.

"We couldn't," I said.

Dylan pulled on my arm. "Yes, we can, Maddie. I bet she has a toilet and everything."

The woman couldn't hide her grin. "I have a toilet, and a sink and a bathtub."

"Could I have a bath?" he asked.

We both spoke at the same time again, only I said no and she said yes.

She held up her hand before I could say anything else. "I'm here all by myself. My husband is off talking about his glory days with his college buddies. There's hot water, and it's not a bother."

Dylan started bouncing up and down. "Please, Maddie, please," he begged.

"Please, Maddie," the woman said with a smile.

All I could think was that it would be so much easier than dragging ourselves all the way over to Tim's.

I nodded. "Thank you," I said.

Dylan cheered, let go of my hand and started for the side door of the RV. The gray-haired woman offered me her hand. "I'm Anna."

"I'm Maddie," I said. "That's Dylan."

The RV was nicer than a lot of houses I'd seen. Anna showed us the bathroom. It was bigger than I expected. I helped Dylan with his teeth and then filled the tub for him. Anna had given him a tiny red boat and a rubber duck, along with two fluffy yellow towels. I washed his hair and told him he had a couple of minutes to play.

Anna offered me a mug as I stepped out of the bath-room. "Hot chocolate," she said.

There were little marshmallows on top. "Thank you," I said. I took a sip. It was hot and chocolaty, made with real milk. I looked through the windshield to see if I could see Q.

"Your brother isn't back yet," Anna said.

She thought Q was my brother. Maybe that was a good thing.

I glanced back over my shoulder. We could hear Dylan splashing in the tub. "I'll clean everything up," I said. "And I'll wash those towels for you."

Anna waved my words away. "Two towels," she said. "That's nothing. I'll toss them in the washer in the morning."

"You have a washer?" I said.

She nodded. "You can do a load in the morning if you'd like."

If I'd like. Yes, I would like. But I wasn't sure it was a good idea to get too friendly.

I glanced at the bathroom again.

"He's okay," Anna said. "Let him play."

"Thank you for letting us use your bathroom," I said, taking another long sip of the hot chocolate. "And for this."

"Oh, you're welcome," she said. "I think it's wonderful that you all stayed together. Do you mind my asking what happened to your parents?"

She thought we were a family—Q, me and Dylan. I swallowed my discomfort. "They're, um…they're gone."

True as far as it went. Dylan's parents were gone. My dad was, and my mother might as well be, and Q didn't seem to have anyone.

"I'm so sorry," Anna said softly.

I gestured over my shoulder. "I'd better get him out," I said. I gave her the cup and went into the bathroom.

Dylan was trying to fit the duck on the boat, which of course just made it sink. "C'mon, kiddo," I said. "Time to get out."

I expected him to complain, but he didn't. Once he was dry, I wiped up the bathroom as much as I could. "Have one last pee," I told him. "And don't forget to wash your hands. I'll be right outside."

I gave Anna one towel, and Dylan brought the other out with him. "Thank you," I said, yet again. I nudged Dylan with a hand against his back.

"Thank you," he said. "I like your bathroom."

"You're welcome," she said.

I wrapped Dylan's jacket around him and hustled him outside before he said something that got us all in trouble.

Q was coming across the empty lot. "Hop into the backseat and wrap up in the blanket before you get cold," I told Dylan as I unlocked the door. I handed him his bag. "Take Fred."

I waited by the front of the car for Q. He shook his head as he got close. "They aren't there." He looked around me. "Is the kid okay?"

"He's fine." I took a step toward him and lowered my voice. "Q, his pajamas and toothbrush were in that bag with his teddy bear."

Q wiped a hand over his neck. "I'm not surprised. They were at the hospital, but only long enough to get a prescription."

It felt like I'd just swallowed a rock. "They left him on purpose."

Q closed his eyes and nodded.

"What do we do?" I looked back at Dylan, who waved at me. I waggled my fingers at him and then turned back to Q.

"For tonight, nothing," he said. "We'll keep him with us. We'll figure it out in the morning."

For the first time, I noticed how tired he seemed. "Thank you for trying to find them," I said.

He jammed his hands in his pockets. "You know, I knew the guy was a prick. I just didn't know he was this big of a one."

"Did you find my mom?" Dylan asked the moment Q opened the driver's door.

Q smiled at him. "Your mom wants you to stay with us for a while."

Dylan nodded slowly. "She put my pajamas in my bag."

"I like them," Q said. "Are you warm enough?"

"Uh-huh," Dylan said. "I had a bath."

Q looked at me, confused. Before I could explain, Dylan pointed at the brown RV over Q's shoulder. "We went over there. Can we get a house on wheels like that?"

"Maybe someday," I said. I leaned over the seat and fished out another blanket from the box where Q kept them. "It's time to go to sleep," I told him.

"Where?" Dylan said.

That was the question.

"Up here," Q said. He reached under the seat and tilted the back. "Okay, c'mon up."

I got Dylan and the blankets out of the backseat while Q unfolded the cardboard screen. Then we made a bed for Dylan in the driver's seat. It only worked because he was little.

Dylan reached for my hand. "Maddie, where're you gonna be?"

I pointed at the passenger seat. "Right there beside you." I kissed the top of his head. "Go to sleep," I said.

Q had put up the wall between the front and backseats. "I have to walk over to Tim's," I said. "I need to use the bathroom."

"It's too dark," Q said.

"Yeah, well, I still gotta pee. And we can't leave him here."

Q looked around. "Ask her." He dipped his head toward the RV.

I shook my head. "No. I've walked all over the place at night. I can take care of myself."

"I know that," Q said. He pointed at the car. "But he needs you...and so do I."

We stood there staring at each other, and then Q wiggled his eyebrows at me.

I shook my head. "Fine. If you're going to get all spazzy about it."

"Thank you," he said.

"She thinks we're brothers and sister." I waved a finger back and forth between us.

Q nodded. "Got it."

I knocked on the RV door. She opened it so quickly, she'd had to be close by. "Anna, umm, could I, umm, use your bathroom?" I asked. I held my breath, hoping she'd say no, because this was a bad, bad idea.

"Of course." She took a step back. "Come in."

As I made my way to the bathroom, I could hear horror movie music playing in my head. All I needed was for Anna to figure out the way things really were, and we were so screwed. Lucky for me, she wasn't all that savvy about things. I mean, there were a couple of teenagers and a little kid sleeping in an old car next to her big fancy RV. Didn't that make her wonder what the heck was going on?

"You can have a bath, Maddie, if you'd like one," Anna said.

If I'd like one. Yes, I'd love to lie in that little tub and use those big, soft towels. I'd like to use some of the shampoo on the shelf that smelled like coconut and maybe some of the lotion. But. I. Couldn't.

"No, thank you," I said, ducking into the bathroom before she had a chance to push.

I peed, brushed my teeth and washed my face. I looked at the tub and then made myself look away, because if I got too friendly with Anna, the next thing that would happen would be I'd be back with my mother and Evan smacking me across the face every time I didn't feel the Holy Spirit. I thanked Anna and got the heck out of there.

Q was leaning against the front fender of the car. "Can we move the car without her hearing?" I asked, keeping my voice low.

His eyes narrowed. "Why? What did she say to you?"

I scuffed my boot on the pavement. "Nothing. She's just too nice. She thinks we're a family, but she never once asked me why we're sleeping in the car. I don't—" I stopped. How was I going to explain this? "It doesn't feel right, Q. Please, can we go?"

Q studied my face for a long moment. "Okay. But we should wait until closer to morning. Do you really want to wake up the kid?"

I studied Dylan through the car window, curled up with the old brown bear.

"What are we going to do?" I said. "I don't think they're coming back."

"Maybe they'll show up in the morning," Q said.

I kicked a piece of broken pavement. It went skittering under the car. "You don't really believe that, do you?"

Q kicked the tire with the heel of his boot. "No. I know it's possible, but I don't think it's very likely."

I jammed my hands in my pockets. "What'll happen to Dylan?"

Q frowned at me and shook his head very slightly. "What do you mean?"

"Do we take him to the police or one of the shelters or what?"

"We keep him with us."

My mouth probably fell open, I was so surprised. "What do you mean, we keep him with us? Are you crazy?"

Q ran a hand over his mouth before he spoke. "First of all, if we take Dylan to the police or even one of the shelters, you think they're not going to ask a lot of questions about us? Whatever you left, do you wanna go back? Do you even want to see your so-called family? Because I don't."

I stared at my feet, feeling the panic I'd been trying to keep pushed down pushing back. "Couldn't we—I don't know—take him somewhere? The hospital? A fire station?"

"The kid's not a library book you forgot to take back, Maddie," Q said. He sounded tired.

It had gotten so dark that I could barely see his face. "I know that," I said. "But how the hell are we going to take care of him?"

"We'll figure something out," Q said. "Anything we do would be better than foster care. You want him yelled at, smacked around...or worse?"

I closed my eyes. For a second, I could feel Evan's hand connect with my face, all of his force, all of his anger behind it. It was so real for a moment that I put my hand up to the side of my head. "No," I whispered.

"Then we keep him," Q said. "Let's get some sleep. We'll work it out in the morning."

I didn't see how we could work it out in the morning or any other time, but I was so tired, I couldn't think of anything else to do. I rolled up in my blankets on the passenger seat of the car. Q got settled in the back. I thought about my prayer in church that morning, how I'd asked God to take care of Dylan. Was this his idea? Did he think that Q and I would be better family for the little guy than the one he had?

Or maybe God hadn't heard me at all. Maybe all the other prayers had been louder than mine.

"It'll be all right, Maddie," Q's voice said from the backseat.

"I hope so," I whispered back.

eight

It was very early and very dark when Q touched my cheek and whispered my name. I bumped my elbow on the crank for the window as I sat up, my legs tangled in the blanket.

"I'm sorry," he said. "Do you still want to get out of here?"

There were a few stars winking at me overhead. I looked over at the RV beside us. It was dark and still. "Yes," I said.

"Can you steer from there?"

"Not really."

Q sighed and pulled down the blanket hanging between us. "Is there any way you can move the kid over without waking him up?"

Dylan had slid down and was curled up on the seat like a little caterpillar. "I don't know," I said. "Maybe."

I pushed my blankets between the seats and pushed myself onto the floor, the dashboard digging into my back. I slid one hand around Dylan and one under him and lifted him over into my seat. It wouldn't have worked, except that he was so small. He shifted and made soft whimpering noises like a puppy, but he didn't wake up. Q gave me one of the blankets, and I tucked it around Dylan.

"Okay, that's good," Q said. "Can you get out from that side?"

I could and I did. Q pushed the driver's seat forward and climbed out of the car. He walked around to me. His face was dark with stubble, and he looked like he hadn't slept at all. He stood right in front of me and spoke in a low voice.

"Here's what we're going to do. I'm going to push by the driver's door so I can steer through the window. You go round to the back and push. We're on a bit of a slope, so we should be able to do it."

I nodded.

He pointed across the lot to the All-mart entrance. "We'll keep going until we get to that speed bump by the main doors."

"Got it," I said. It was cold, and my legs were stiff from sleeping in the passenger seat all night. Wanting to get away from Anna's trailer was probably wacko of me, but I needed to do it.

Q put the car in neutral and then rolled down the left front window. I braced my hands on the trunk. He lifted his left hand and dropped it, and I started to push. The pavement was damp, and my feet slipped for a second before they found traction. The muscles in my back and shoulders tied themselves into knots, but I kept on pushing. Nothing happened. The car didn't move.

I pushed with everything I had, biting the inside of my cheek so I wouldn't grunt out loud. I could see Q's shape in front of me, knees bent, shoulders straining. And then slowly the car began to roll forward, tires making a creeping sound on the asphalt.

The speed bump was more or less level with the *t* at the end of All-mart, and I kept my eyes locked on that red letter as my arms and legs kept the car moving forward. Just before the hump of pavement, I lifted my hands and stepped back from the car. The tires bumped the rise, and the car stopped moving forward.

Q opened the door, pressed hard on the brake, just in case, and put it into park. He pulled his head out of the car and grinned at me. "We did it, Maddie," he said.

Without thinking, I flung my arms around him. And immediately felt very weird. I let go and took an awkward step back. And like he always seemed to do, Q somehow felt how weird I felt.

He reached over and tugged the zipper on my jacket the rest of the way up. "S'okay," he said softly. "Let's get out of here."

I climbed into the backseat. Q got behind the wheel and started the car, circling the mall and heading for Tim's. Dylan had slept through the whole thing.

"Watch for cop cars," Q warned. "I don't want to get caught with him not in a car seat or without even a seatbelt."

But we made it. As we pulled into the overflow lot at Tim's, I could feel the panic floating away.

"Coffee?" Q asked. He pulled off his hat and tossed it onto the dash.

"I think we've earned it. Do we have the money for it?"

Q parked next to a picnic table at the back of the lot. We got out of the car, and Q went to get us two coffees. We sat on top of the table, our feet on the bench seat. I could easily see Dylan, still curled up on the passenger seat.

Q followed my eyes. "Maddie, I don't think his family is coming back."

Neither did I. I set my cup down between my feet and tucked my fingers in my armpits to warm them a bit. "How could they leave him?" I asked.

Q exhaled slowly. "I don't think Michael thinks about anyone but himself."

"But why Dylan? Why not the baby or the other little guy?"

"I don't know. Maybe because he's the oldest of the three. He'd eat more, and he probably asked more questions." He shifted his coffee from one hand to the other. "Maybe he went eeny meeny miny mo, for all I know."

I picked up my own cup. "Are you serious about us keeping him?"

"Absolutely," he said.

"I don't know if I can," I said.

Dylan stirred, sat up and looked around in a panic. I was off the picnic bench almost before my brain had a chance to tell my feet to move. I opened the car door and put my arms around him. "It's okay, kiddo," I said. "I'm right here."

He was crying—no sound, just huge heaving shudders against my chest. It felt like a knife, slicing out a piece of my heart. He clutched fistfuls of my jacket with each hand. I pressed my face against the top of his head. Q had come to stand beside the open car door. I looked up at him in the faint light. "I'll do it," I said.

I took Dylan for a pee and washed his face. He didn't say much, but he wouldn't let go of my hand.

When I came out, Q had gone into Tim's and had bought me a new cup of coffee as well as a breakfast sandwich, and there was a sandwich for Dylan and a bottle of apple juice. We took a table in the corner. Dylan watched the early morning delivery trucks in the drive-through. He ate with one hand, still clinging tightly to mine with the other.

"We need a place to live," Q said in a low voice. "The three of us can't stay in the car."

"We can't afford an apartment."

He wrapped his hands around his paper cup. "I know, but maybe a room."

"So how are we going to pay for this room?" I asked. I set down my cup and pulled a bit of egg out of my sandwich.

Q touched the front of his jacket. "I have the money I made last week."

I thought about my emergency fund and my go-back-to-school money. Dylan's hand was warm in mine. I looked at him as he slowly chewed his sandwich and watched a milk delivery truck go past the window. "I have some money," I said.

"Okay, so what we need is a place." Q propped his elbows on the table. "I might have an idea."

"What?"

"John Goddard."

I picked up my cup. "The guy you worked for last week."

He nodded.

"The guy you called a cheap asshole."

"Yeah." He drank the last of his coffee. "I know he has a couple of rental places, and I don't think he's the type of guy to be real picky about who he rents to." Q looked over at Dylan. "I don't think he'd ask a lot of questions."

"That would be good," I said.

"I'll go over to where we were last week. I think they're going to start there this morning." He glanced at Dylan again. "Will you guys be all right?"

"Yeah, we'll go over to the mall. We can walk around, and I can even push him in a cart." I pulled a slice of cold bacon out of my sandwich and ate it. Q reached across the table, broke off a piece of the top biscuit and popped it into his mouth.

I leaned over to Dylan. "Have some more juice, kiddo," I said. "We're leaving soon."

He turned. "Okay," he said softly.

I handed him the bottle.

"I'll drive you over," Q said.

"You sure?" I asked.

His face softened into a smile. "Uh-huh. It's too cold for the two of you to walk. We'll go in about ten minutes." He stood up. "I'll be right back." He headed in the direction of the washrooms.

My coffee was cold, but I drank it anyway.

Dylan set his juice bottle on the table. He looked around and sighed.

"Wanna come sit on my lap?" I asked.

He nodded, and I picked him up. He leaned his head against me, and I wrapped my arms around him. I'd never much liked all the huggy, kissy stuff—not that my mom was much for it—but I didn't mind keeping Dylan close at all.

We stayed like that until Q came back. He smiled at us and put both hands on the table. "Ready to go?" he asked.

"Do you need to pee again?" I asked Dylan.

"No," he said.

There were lots of bathrooms at the mall, I figured. "We're ready," I said. I set Dylan down, and right away he reached for my hand. "Just let me put my jacket on," I told him.

As soon as my hand was through the sleeve, he grabbed it. We headed out to the car. "I'm gonna sit in the back with him," I told Q.

"Good idea," he said.

We drove back to the mall. It was starting to feel, well, okay, not like home but kind of like our place.

"I don't know how long I'll be," Q said. "I'll find you."

"Okay," I said.

"It'll be okay," he said.

I nodded and stepped away from the car. The mall was quiet. The stores were still closed, although the mall walkers were already out. "Let's go find the giraffe," I said to Dylan. He was holding on to me with one hand and the grocery bag with Fred in it with the other.

He looked up at me, frowning. "Maddie, where are we going to sleep tonight?" he asked in a small voice.

"Probably in the car like last night," I said.

His eyes went from me to the big doors we'd just come through and back again. "But Q took the car," he said.

I crouched down to his level. "He's coming back," I said.

"No, he's not." He stared down at his feet instead of at me. "My mom didn't come back."

I didn't know how to do this. "Dylan. It's not the same thing. Your mom would come if she could." Was it wrong to say that? I took a deep breath. "She would never leave you.

I bet she has a good reason, and when she does come back, she'll tell us what it is."

His lower lip quivered. "I was bad," he whispered.

I threw my arms around him. "You were not bad," I said. My mother had told me I was bad more than once, and maybe she was right, because, after all, here I was in a mall at eight o'clock in the morning with someone else's kid, living in a car with a guy I only met last week. But Dylan was not bad. His father was a total prick, but I couldn't exactly say that, could I?

"You are the best, best, best kid," I said. "And Q will be back, I promise."

I broke out of the hug, fished out one of the napkins I'd stuffed in my pocket, and wiped his face. "Let's find the giraffe," I said.

We started down the mall. I couldn't help glancing back at the mall entrance. Q *would* come back. Wouldn't he? He had the car. He had money. My stomach started to tie itself into a knot. *Don't be stupid*, I told myself. *Q's coming back. He's not like Dylan's jerk-off of a father.*

I wanted to go back to the doors and look outside. I don't know what I thought I'd see…maybe Q in the parking lot, getting ready to hit the road? I felt, I don't know, trapped in the mall, like if I could just get outside, I could somehow make Q come back. Right—and if I went racing for the parking lot, I'd scare the crap out of Dylan.

Just then Dylan pulled on my hand. He'd spotted the giraffe. We headed for it, and there was nothing I could do except go climb on a big pink-and-purple giraffe and hope things were going to work out.

Dylan was playing in the helicopter next to the food courts when Q found us. He touched my shoulder, and I wanted to fling my arms around him, but I'd already done that and it just made things weird between us. I held up a finger and leaned inside the helicopter to nudge Dylan.

"See?" I said. "I told you Q would come back."

He leaned around me to see for himself. Q smiled and did his spazzy eyebrow thing, which made us all laugh.

"Q and I are going to sit right here on this bench," I said. "Okay?"

"Don't go anywhere," Dylan said, but he didn't reach for my hand. That had to be good.

"I won't," I promised. I dropped onto the padded seat next to Q. "He's got this thing that I'll leave him."

"Can you blame him?" Q said.

I watched Dylan showing Fred how to move the levers and push the buttons. "No, not really." I shifted sideways and pulled one leg up underneath me. "So," I said. "Did you find the guy?"

Q nodded, and I could see the start of a smile on his face.

"So tell me," I said, giving him a punch on the shoulder.

"He has a room in a building downtown. It doesn't sound very big, but it has its own bathroom."

"Its own bathroom. You're sure? Not some grotty thing we have to share with strangers?"

"I'm sure," Q said. He reached in his jacket pocket and pulled out a key ring with two silver keys on it. "We can go see it if you want. Before I give him any money."

Dylan was making *vroom, vroom* noises in the helicopter. I suddenly realized that with a real address, I could get a library card. The first thing I was going to get was a book about trains and another about helicopters for Dylan.

I turned back to Q. "How much money?"

He sighed. "Hundred a week. Cash every Saturday."

I shook my head. "It's too much."

He unzipped his jacket and leaned forward, hand hanging between his legs. "We aren't going to find anything better, Maddie," he said. "Shit! We aren't going to find anything as good. As long as he gets his money, Goddard won't ask any questions about you, about me, about the kid."

I raked my fingers back through my hair. "We don't have a hundred dollars a week. Between the two of us, we wouldn't even make it two months."

"Goddard offered me a job," Q said. "Off the books. Cash."

I looked at him, not quite sure what to say. On the one hand, it was the answer to a prayer—if I had actually prayed for help, which I hadn't. On the other hand, it was pretty clear John Goddard was a sleazebag who took advantage of people who didn't have a lot of other choices. Like us. "Are you taking it?" I asked finally.

"I already said I would," he said. He held up a hand, but I wasn't going to object. "It's the best choice for now, Maddie.

We'll have some place to live. The three of us can't stay in the car. Once we get ahead a little, I'll find a real job. It's just for now, I promise."

"I can keep collecting bottles," I said.

He nodded. "And we should be able to keep getting food from the hotel at least a couple of times a week." He looked down at his feet. "There's one other thing," he said.

"What?" My stomach started retying the knot that had loosened when Q had touched my shoulder.

"I'm getting rid of the car."

I straightened up. "No."

"It's a done deal," he said.

"So, make it an undone deal," I said. "That's your car. It's your, your…" I gestured with both hands. "It's your place."

Q put one hand on the top of his head. He looked beat. "The room—the building is right downtown. There's no parking. We need the room way more than we need the car. I can get a lift or take the bus or even hitch to get to work, and downtown, you can get everywhere you need to go."

I leaned all the way back against the bench. "You sold it to Goddard, didn't you?" I said.

Q didn't say a thing, which was as good as saying yes.

"He's going to give you nothing for it and then turn around and sell it to someone for probably three times as much."

"We need the money."

"He's ripping you off!"

"The world is like that sometimes, Maddie," Q said. "You'd better get used to it."

Dylan climbed out of the helicopter then, holding Fred in one hand. He came and stood in front of Q. "I need to pee, and so does Fred," he said. "Will you take us? Fred doesn't like to pee around girls."

Q looked down at the bear with a totally straight face. "Fred, my man, I know exactly how you feel." He held out a hand to Dylan, who took it.

Dylan looked at me. "We'll be back, Maddie, promise."

Something in his face made my chest ache, but I smiled and said, "Okay."

By the time Q and Dylan—and Fred—came back, the mall stores were open. I'd got the bag Dylan had left in the helicopter ride and was waiting for them, leaning against the back of the bench.

"Wanna go look at the place?" Q asked.

"Okay," I said.

Dylan let go of Q's hand and reached for mine. "Where are we going?" he asked.

"To look at a place where maybe all three of us can live," I said.

"Is it a van?"

I looked at Q over the top of Dylan's head. A van. His only thought of somewhere to live was a van. I couldn't speak because I was suddenly overwhelmed with the idea of hunting down Michael and beating on him with my backpack.

"No, not a van," Q said. "A room, a little apartment with our own bathroom."

We started for the mall doors.

"Just for us, or other people too?" Dylan asked.

"Just us."

He hugged the bear to his chest. "Fred doesn't like those places where everybody sleeps together."

"You mean the shelter?" Q asked.

Dylan shrugged. "I don't know. There were a lot of people, and some of them weren't very nice. So my dad said we should just all sleep in the van, but it was kind of cold."

"This place will be warm," Q promised. He turned away, and I could see he was gritting his teeth.

When I was at church, I thought about praying to God to take care of Dylan. Had it only been yesterday morning? Maybe this was his answer. Maybe it was his plan for Q and me to take care of the kid. I was starting to sound like the Holy Rollers. But just in case God was listening, I sent out a silent prayer:

Dear God,

Please take care of Dylan's mom and the other kids, and if you could give his father a really itchy rash on his privates, that would be good too.

Amen

nine

The room was filthy. Not dirty like the people who had lived in it were pigs: dirty like actual pigs had lived there.

"Maddie, it smells bad," Dylan said. "I don't like it here." He leaned against me, and I put my hand on the top of his head. I looked at Q.

"I'm sorry," he said. "I had no idea it would be like this. I'll take the key back and tell Goddard to forget it." He started for the stairs.

I grabbed his sleeve. "Don't."

He looked at me like I was nuts. "We can't live in that," he said. "It's too dirty for bugs. You wouldn't even get a rat in a place like this."

It smelled like puke and people who hadn't washed. But there was a big window that let the sun in and an old tub with feet in the small bathroom. "I can clean it," I said.

Q shook his head. "No. There's gotta be a better choice."

Except I knew there wasn't. Who was going to rent anything to a couple of teenagers and a kid? Nobody. Now it was me shaking my head. "It has to be here, Q," I said. "It's better than no place."

He slid both hands up over his face and down the back of his head. "Okay. What do you need?"

I'd cleaned the house a lot when I lived at home because it wasn't really my mom's thing. She'd walk over something on the floor rather than pick it up. I didn't know if she just didn't see the dirt, or she didn't care. I saw it and I did care, so I learned to clean it up. "Can we go to the grocery store?" I asked. "I need a bucket and some kind of cleaner—oh yeah, and a big jug of bleach."

I loved the smell of bleach the way some people got off on nail polish or paint. I don't mean I went around sniffing the bottle and being all weird, just that it made me feel better, like everything had been sanitized for my protection.

See, I had this thing about germs. They scared the crap out of me. My dad had gotten pneumonia, and while he was in the hospital he caught some other germ. They called it a superbug. He died because the germ was stronger than the doctors, stronger than their drugs, stronger than my dad.

I spent my emergency fund on cleaning supplies. Dylan wouldn't go to the park without me, so Q brought in a blanket and we put him out in the hall by the open door.

Q got the window open, which helped with the smell, and then he swept the floor, which helped even more. I started washing the walls, and the smell of bleach pushed out the smell of rotting food and vomit pretty quickly.

I washed everything in the main room—the walls, the door, the doorknob. Then I washed my way across the floor to the hall. My hands were red and cracked in a couple of places from the bleach. Q looked at them and winced.

"I'm hungry," Dylan announced.

"Me too," I said. I put my arm around him and messed up his hair. "Let's go get some lunch."

I pulled on my jacket. "Soup line?" I said to Q.

"Are you sure?" he asked.

I bent to zip up Dylan's jacket. "The food's decent, and it's not junk. And the price is right."

"Okay," he said. "I should be able to get supper from the hotel tonight."

"That would be good," I said. I mimicked his eyebrow thing. He laughed. I took Dylan's hand and headed for the stairs.

Q was walking on the outside, closest to the street, and a lot slower than he usually walked, so Dylan didn't have to run to keep up. I smiled down at him, and he smiled back. Then he leaned around me to look at Q. "You should hold Maddie's hand," he said.

"Okay," Q said.

I felt weird taking Q's hand, especially when mine were all dried out from cleaning. Like Dylan's, Q's hand was warm holding mine. His fingers were long and strong, calloused from the rough work he'd been doing. All this hand-holding felt strange—not bad, just not me. But then I wasn't exactly sure who *me* was anymore.

I wasn't the person Evan claimed was going to hell, although I might be a whole lot closer to ending up there. I wasn't the person who'd run away. I wasn't even the person Q had met a week ago. I didn't know who I was, and for now that was going to have to be okay, because I didn't have time to figure it out.

Lunch was a chicken stir-fry with rice. There were brownies for dessert, and I wrapped mine carefully in a paper napkin so Dylan could have it later.

The room looked a lot better now that it was clean, and God knows it smelled way better. Dylan walked around showing everything to Fred while Q and I stood in the bathroom doorway. Whoever had been in the room before had had a dog and hadn't been too picky about taking it out for a walk.

"It smells like a toilet," I said to Q.

"I think whoever—or whatever—lived here used the floor as a toilet," he said. He grimaced. "What do you want me to do?"

I looked around. "I don't know," I said. "Shovel it out, I guess."

He used the broom and a couple of pieces of cardboard to scrape the crap off the floor. Again, I washed everything. Dylan fell asleep on the blanket in a square of sunshine in front of the window. Three of my knuckles were bleeding by the time I was done.

"Shit, Maddie," Q said. "Enough. This place is cleaner than a hospital."

I sat back on my heels. "We need something to sleep on," I said.

"I've got a sleeping bag in the car," he said. "I didn't use it because it's kind of small, but it should work for the kid." He made a fist with his hand and beat the end of it slowly against his mouth. "How about a couple of those floaty blow-up things, you know, to lay on?"

I nodded. "Yeah. You mean air mattresses."

I was going to have to go to the thrift store for clothes for Dylan and maybe a couple more blankets, but I didn't like to buy anything that I couldn't wash. I'd gotten him some Spiderman underwear, a pair of socks and a slightly too large pair of sweatpants out of a seventy-percent-off bin at the grocery store. I'd also gotten two hideous orange towels. I thought about lying down in that tub until the water was up to my nose.

"There's that discount store up the hill," Q said. "I'll try there. And I need to go give Goddard the money." He pulled a bottle of juice out of his pocket. "It's warm, sorry."

"Did you swipe that at lunchtime?" I asked. My hair was coming loose, so I pulled out the elastic and finger-combed it back from my face.

"I don't think they'll go broke over one bottle of juice." He held out his hand and I got to my feet, following him into the other room, where Dylan was still asleep.

"Should I wake him up?" I asked.

"Let him sleep," he said. "I think he's worn-out. I'll be back soon."

I nodded.

Q paused in the doorway. "I like your hair like that," he said. Then he was gone.

Okay, so what did that mean? Did he mean like, as in my hair looked better loose than it did in a ponytail? Or did he mean like, as in he liked me? And why did I even care? Q and I weren't like that. Not that it would be a bad thing. But we were friends. Nothing more.

I stretched out on the edge of the blanket next to Dylan and leaned my head against the wall. Did Q think we were something else? I'd held his hand when we'd gone for lunch, but that was because of Dylan. And I had hugged him, but that was only the once.

The next thing I knew, Dylan was sitting on my chest, poking my cheek with his finger. I opened my right eye and focused it on him. He giggled.

"Maddie, open your other eye," he demanded.

I made a show of trying and failing to get my left eye open. "It's stuck," I said.

He frowned and poked my left temple with a finger. I made that side of my face twitch.

"Do that again," I said.

Dylan jabbed my face once more.

I did the twitchy thing again. "I think it's working." I grunted and fluttered my eyelid. Then I opened the eye. "You did it, Dylan," I told him. I swallowed him up in a hug and he laughed, throwing his arms around my neck. I put my mouth against the outside of his arm and made a loud, slurpy mouth fart. That sent him into a squirm of laughter again.

I did it again, just to hear him laugh. It was a great sound. Then I lifted him up and settled him sideways on my lap. "You want a drink?" I asked.

He nodded. I unscrewed the cap and handed him the bottle. He took a long drink. "I'm hungry," he said.

Keeping one arm around him, I leaned right and snagged the strap of my backpack with one finger. I fished inside and found the napkin-wrapped brownie.

"Here," I said.

He broke the brownie into three pieces. "One for me, one for Fred, one for Maddie."

He fed Fred his bite, and helped with the eating. I made Fred rub his furry stomach and bow his thanks to Dylan.

Then Dylan and I ate our pieces. "Can I have a drink of your juice?" I asked.

He nodded, and I took a long drink. It was way too warm for me, but it didn't seem like a good idea to say that in front of a kid.

I put the cap back on the bottle and stashed it in the side pocket of my pack.

Dylan put an arm around Fred and settled back against my chest. "It smells better in here," he said.

"That's because it's clean now."

"Are we going to live here?" he asked.

"Uh-huh," I said.

"Where are we going to sleep?"

I pointed to the wall opposite. "There. Q's gone to get us something to sleep on."

"And nobody else gets to sleep here?"

"Nobody." I made an X on my chest. "Cross my heart."

He sighed softly.

"How about tomorrow we go to the thrift store and see if we can find some toys for Fred to play with?" I said.

"Can we look for a train?"

"Sure."

"And crayons?"

"Why not?"

We were talking about our favorite colors when Q got back. He was carrying a large plastic bag from the discount store, so I was pretty sure he'd found the air mattresses. "You find them?" I asked.

He nodded and handed me the bag. "Lime green and two orange ones."

I grinned. "Hey, they'll go with our towels." I pulled the plastic packages out of the bag. "What color, kiddo?" I said to Dylan.

"Green," he said.

"Okay," I said. I took out the green air mattress, unfolded it and started to blow it up. Q had already started on one of the others. It takes a lot of air to blow up one of those things, I discovered. I had to stop twice—once because I got dizzy and almost fell over sideways, making Dylan giggle again.

But we finally got them all blown up. Dylan—and Fred—stretched out on the green mattress that Q had tucked in one corner of the room. He rolled around, and I hoped the damn thing wouldn't pop.

"Fred likes it," he said.

"Good," I said. "Just tell him not to bounce too hard or there's going to be a giant pop in here."

"We need to empty the car," Q said. "Goddard wants it in the morning."

"Of course," I said. He let the sarcasm go.

I'd only spent a few nights sleeping in the Honda, and it wasn't even my car in the first place, so why did I feel all squirmy about Q selling it to John Goddard? I'd never cared about stuff before, probably because after my dad died, my mom and I had moved a lot. Sometimes it was because of money, and other times it was just because she got bored.

We lugged all the boxes up the stairs, stacking them under the window. I couldn't help yawning as I set the last box on the pile.

"I'm gonna go get our supper," Q said. "Just, I don't know, just do nothing until I get back."

Kinda hard to do nothing with Dylan there. Fred wanted to try all three of the air mattresses, so I told Dylan the story of "Goldilocks and the Three Bears." Except it had been a long time since I'd heard the story, so some of the "Three Little Pigs" sort of got mixed in too, but nobody seemed to mind.

Q came back with steak, baked potato and something that looked like lime-green cauliflower.

"That looks yucky," Dylan said.

"What is it?" I said to Q.

"I don't know," he said, spearing a piece with his plastic fork. "Mmm, it's good, though." He looked at Dylan sitting next to me with Fred beside him on the floor, a takeout spoon in the teddy bear's lap. "Tell Fred it's got lots of cheese sauce. He can close his eyes if he doesn't want to look at it."

I was ready for Dylan to pitch a fit, but he took a small bit of the green stuff and lots of the sauce and tried a bite.

"So," Q said. "What does Fred think?"

"He likes it," Dylan said.

"Yeah, the bear's a gourmet," Q said with a grin.

"What's a gor...gor..."

"A gourmet," I said.

"What is it?" Dylan asked, spearing another piece of the green cauliflower.

"Someone who knows about food," Q said.

Dylan thought about it for a moment, then nodded and went back to eating.

And it was as easy and comfortable as that. I washed Dylan's hair and then he took a bath while Fred watched from the safety of the top of the toilet tank. I tucked Dylan and the bear into the sleeping bag, and he fell asleep almost at once.

Q touched my arm. "Go have a bath, Maddie."

"I feel like I should be doing something," I said, wiping a hand over my neck.

He reached up and pulled the elastic from my hair. "You should be having a bath," he said. He tipped his head toward the bathroom. "Go before I pick you up and throw you in."

I lay in the water trying to remember the last time I'd had a bath. Before Evan, that was for sure. When he was around, I took showers. It just seemed safer for some reason I couldn't put into words.

I lay awake for a long time on my air mattress. Not that it was uncomfortable. After sleeping in the car, and before that, covered in cardboard in one old building or another, this was like being at a fancy hotel. I just couldn't get my mind to shut off or even slow down. I finally did fall asleep, then woke up with a jolt. I stared into the darkness, remembering where I was and why. Q's mattress was a few feet away. He was on his side, head propped on one hand, watching me.

"Did I wake you up?" I asked, pushing the hair back from my face.

He shook his head. "I was just thinking."

I rolled onto my side and folded an arm under my head. I could hear Dylan, or maybe it was Fred, softly snoring in the corner. "What about?"

"How much my life has changed since you cut out of the Holy Rollers' service."

"I bet you never thought this would happen."

He laughed softly. "When you came flying around the side of the building, I didn't even know if I should talk to you."

"Why?"

"Because you're a girl and I'm a guy, and I'm kinda tall and I was all in black like some vampire and I was sitting there in the dark."

I pulled the blanket up a little higher. "I wasn't scared," I said.

"Really?"

"Okay, maybe when you first spoke to me, but not after that."

Q rolled onto his back. "You mean once you felt the power of my charm."

I gave a snort of laughter. "Yeah, something like that."

We lay there in the dark for a while, and the silence wasn't weird. It was just...there. I thought Q had fallen asleep, but then he spoke. "This is my family now, Maddie. I'm not sorry about anything."

I glanced over at Dylan, just the top of his head sticking out of the sleeping bag. "Do you think they'll come back for him?"

"I don't know." He exhaled slowly. "There's something I should tell you. I asked one of the guys up there who brings in the carts to watch for them. I'll check with him, I don't know, once a week."

"What if they show up?"

"It's up to you."

It was easier to say things in the dark, when Q couldn't see my face and I couldn't see his. "I don't want to give him back," I said in a small, low voice. "Not to Michael anyway."

"Then we won't," Q said.

He stretched a hand out into the space between us. "This is our family, Maddie. The three of us. What happened before now doesn't matter."

I felt in the darkness until I touched his hand. He linked his fingers with mine. The warmth in his hand spread up my arm and into my chest.

"I love you, Maddie," he whispered.

Was that what I was feeling? I'd felt something when I'd hugged Q. And when he'd pulled the elastic out of my hair. Was that love? Did it happen this fast?

He pulled gently on my hand. Not only was it easier to say things in the darkness, it was easier to do things. It was really easy not to think at all. And that's what I did. I stopped thinking. I slid off my air mattress and onto Q's, and he wrapped me against him. I kissed him first, boldly pushing my tongue into his mouth. The heat in my chest spread everywhere.

Then Q was touching me and I was touching him, and my head felt like I'd been spinning around and around and around.

I turned to make sure Dylan was still asleep. Little-kid snores were still coming from the corner.

"You sure?" Q whispered, his breath warm against the side of my mouth.

Was I? I loved Q, or it was something close to love. He loved me. I nodded. He reached over and fumbled in the pocket of his pants for something. Then he pulled me to my feet, reaching down to grab the mattress and a blanket. He dragged them into the bathroom, closed the door and then leaned against it, kissing me, his tongue in my mouth now.

I wrapped my arms around his neck, and he eased me down to the air mattress, stopping to pull his shirt over his head.

I couldn't really see him, and I was glad of that, because it meant he couldn't see me either. I slid my fingers over his arms. I could feel the muscles like they'd been carved out of a piece of stone. He started undoing the buttons on my shirt. I moved my hands down over his chest, and he gasped. I figured that was good, and I lifted my head to kiss him again.

We did it there on the bathroom floor. Everything fit together the way it was supposed to. It wasn't exactly how I thought it would be, but it wasn't awful. After, back in the room, Q moved our mattresses closer together. He fell asleep with his hand on my hip.

I lay there beside him for a while. Then I got up and got the long piece of glass I kept in my jacket pocket. I wrapped it up in the leftover paper napkins from the hotel and stuffed it in the bottom of my backpack.

ten

The early morning sun woke me up, hitting me in the face because I was turned toward the window. I got up to go to the bathroom. What I'd done last night felt kind of like a dream. This wasn't exactly how I'd thought things were going to be.

I washed my face, got dressed and braided my hair. I put on my last clean clothes, or, in the case of my jeans, mostly clean.

I had to do laundry today. And get a library card, now that I had an address. And go forage for more returnable bottles.

It hit me that I was going to have to do all those things with Dylan. And I'd promised we'd go to the thrift store. Okay, so no library card today.

Q was awake, and Dylan was just waking up. Q touched my leg as I went past him. He smiled, and I shot him a quick smile back. I sat on the edge of Dylan's mattress. He gave me a sleepy smile, and I brushed the hair out of his face.

"You hungry?" I asked.

He nodded. "An' I need to pee."

"Go to it then," I said, pointing toward the bathroom. He stood up and made his way across the room, kind of rubber-legged, with the back of his hair standing up.

"Wash your hands," I called after him.

Q stood in the middle of the room, stretching. He was wearing nothing but a pair of gray sweatpants. I could see the muscles I'd run my fingers over the night before. And there was dark curly hair on his chest. I felt a fluttery feeling somewhere below my stomach.

Q reached for my hand and pulled me over to him. "Is everything okay with us?" he asked.

I nodded, then glanced at the closed bathroom door. "I just don't want to—"

"—give the kid the wrong idea," he finished.

I looked at him, surprised, although I should have been used to the way he seemed to read my mind by now. "Yeah."

"Okay, so no mushy stuff when he's around."

"Just until…just for now," I said.

He nodded. Then he shot a quick look at the bathroom door and kissed me on the mouth.

When Dylan came out of the bathroom, I got him a roll, part of my last banana and a bottle of juice Q had stuck on the windowsill all night. It was still pretty cool.

"You want a peanut-butter-and-banana sandwich?" I asked Q. I had a couple of peanut butter packets I'd swiped from our last time at Tim's.

"Yeah," he said. He pulled on his boots while I made it, then took a long drink from the water bottle that was still stashed in the window. He grabbed the sandwich and his jacket. "I gotta go," he said.

Dylan looked up.

Q pointed a finger at him. "I'll be back. Promise."

"Okay," Dylan said.

Q smiled at me. "See you later, Maddie," he said, and he was out the door and gone.

After Dylan and I had both eaten, I shook out the blankets and made our "beds."

"Are we going to ride the giraffe?" Dylan asked.

"Nope," I said. "We're going to go hunting for bottles."

We put on our jackets and shoes, and then I grabbed the garbage bags I'd used for laundry and headed out with Dylan. It was a lot harder collecting bottles with a kid. I'd never noticed before how many questions kids ask. All the time. For every two bottles I picked up, I answered about six questions, and I had to watch him all the time. He was like a crow. Anything shiny caught his attention.

Then, when I had two of the bags full, I realized that was as much as I could take, because I needed a free hand to hold on to Dylan. We dragged our way to the recycling center. I wanted to scream at the little bit of money we'd gotten.

"Can we go home now?" Dylan asked.

"We have to go get you some clothes, remember?" I said. He made a face.

"And we're going to look for a truck."

"You said a train," he said.

I had to turn my back and take a couple of deep breaths so I wouldn't scream. "Yeah, we'll look for a train," I said. "After clothes."

I managed to find three pairs of kids' pants. Dylan tried on the first pair, but I couldn't get him to try the others. I didn't want him to pitch a fit in the store, so I just eyeballed them. I figured it didn't really matter so much about shirts, so I just looked at him and guessed.

He'd found a plastic train, the kind of thing you'd get for much younger kids, but it was a train and that was what mattered. And I got a big bag of wooden blocks for fifty cents. We carried it all back to the room, and I washed the train in the sink before I let Dylan play with it. Then I cleaned the bathroom a bit while he drove the train around the room and up over the air mattresses.

It wasn't until he said, "I'm hungry," that I remembered I hadn't figured out lunch. A lot of the time, I only had two meals a day, but he was a kid. I didn't want to do the soup line without Q. I thought about the other choices, not that there were that many. Then I remembered that the church next to the old hospital handed out bag lunches a couple of days a week.

Dylan didn't want to walk. I knew we needed to get there before all the lunches were gone.

"Fine," I said. "I'll carry you partway, but you have to walk partway."

For a little guy, he was heavy. And my arms were tired from carrying the two bags of bottles. I lugged him two blocks and then set him down. "You have to walk for a bit," I told him.

He sat down on the sidewalk. "My feet hurt."

"Well, my arms hurt," I snapped. I sat down beside him, propping my arms on my bent knees. We sat there for a couple of minutes. Out of the corner of my eyes I could see Dylan watching me.

"I'm hungry," he finally said in a small voice.

I felt like a shit. But I couldn't carry him all the way. I nudged him with my shoulder. "I know you are," I said. "But you have to walk. I can't carry you. My arms will fall off."

He frowned, his forehead wrinkled. "Arms can't fall off."

"Well, then mine will be the first." I got to my feet and held out a hand to him. C'mon, let's go. I'm hungry too and I don't want to sit on the sidewalk. It's cold."

For a minute he just sat there, and I thought he was going to have a tantrum. Then he took my hand and stood up.

That didn't mean I'd won. He walked—no, he dragged his feet—all the way to the church. I ground my teeth together to keep from yanking on his arm and pulling him behind me all the way. It had been easier to get two bags of bottles to the recycling center than it was to get Dylan to the church.

We got the last two bag lunches. Now the question was, where the heck were we going to eat?

There was a low stone wall surrounding the parking lot. Dylan was busy looking inside his bag so I was able to walk him over instead of drag him over to the wall.

I brushed off the top and lifted him up, then scrambled up beside him. The top was flat enough to use as a picnic table. We each had a juice box, crackers and cheese, an apple, a banana, a granola bar and a box of raisins. I split one banana for the two of us, saving the rest of the fruit. Dylan ate his own crackers and cheese along with some of mine. I had the rest of the crackers, a bit of banana and one of the granola bars. I packed up everything else into one of the bags to have later and stuffed it into my backpack.

"Where are we going now?" he asked, and I had to do the teeth-clenching thing so I wouldn't get mad at him.

"Home," I said.

He took my hand without saying a word, but he was dragging his feet again. I could have crawled on my stomach along the sidewalk and gone faster. I stopped about a block from the church, folding my arms across my chest.

"Dylan, c'mon," I said. "It's going to take us all afternoon to get there."

"My legs can't go any faster," he said stubbornly.

I pulled my hand back through my hair. This wasn't working. I took off my backpack and put it back on backward so it was against my chest. Then I bent down in front of Dylan. "Climb on," I said.

"Piggyback?" he asked suspiciously.

"Yes, piggyback," I said, hating the tone of my voice. "Just this one time."

He put his arms around my neck and I looped my arms under his legs, boosting him up onto my back.

When I stood up, I almost fell over. I hiked Dylan up a little higher, and while he didn't get any lighter, at least I didn't feel like I was going to drop him on the sidewalk. I started walking, trying not to think about the pain in both my shoulders.

"This isn't how we go home," Dylan said suddenly in my ear.

"How do you know that?" I wheezed.

"Because there's a mailbox, then a big tree and then lights for crossing the street."

Crap! The kid didn't miss much. I didn't know if that was bad.

"We're not going home," I said. "We're going back to the thrift store."

"Why?"

I stopped to look both ways before I crossed the street. Dylan leaned forward to see, and we almost pitched into the street. "Dylan!" I snapped. "Don't do that."

We crossed and kept on in the direction of the thrift store. I didn't know how I was going to walk three more blocks. "Sing me a song," I said.

"No," he muttered against my neck.

"Please," I said. "Pretty please with peanut butter and banana."

"Not peanut butter and banana," he said indignantly. "It's pretty please with sugar on top."

"Sorry," I said. "Pretty please with sugar on top."

Nothing. My back was wet with sweat.

Then I heard Dylan's voice, soft in my ear. "The wheels on the train go 'round and 'round, 'round and 'round, 'round and 'round."

I was pretty sure those were the wrong words, but what the hell did it matter? The train wheels went around, and we finally made it to the store.

I stopped in the empty lot behind the thrift store and let Dylan slip off my back. Then I pulled off my backpack.

"Why are we here?" he asked as we walked around the building.

"I can't carry you all the time," I said. "We need a wagon, a cart, something."

"A wagon," he said.

"Let's see what there is first," I told him as I reached for the door handle.

What there was, was nothing. No wagons. No wire shopping carts I'd seen some people at Pax House with. I would have been happy with a skateboard. We came out and I kicked the garbage can just outside of the door. Dylan looked at me wide-eyed, and I knew I'd gone too far.

I bent down to his level. "I shouldn't have done that," I said. "I'm sorry."

"Are you mad at me?" he asked.

So did I say, *Yes, I'm mad because you won't walk and I can't get anything done and I have to carry you all over this freakin' city?* How many times had I heard, *This is your fault, Maddie?*

I took a breath. I let it out, took another one and did the same thing. Didn't make me feel one bit less pissed. "I'm not mad at you, kiddo," I said. "I'm mad because we couldn't find a wagon. And I'm mad because my feet are tired." I reached over and pushed his hair away from his face, and suddenly it wasn't so hard to smile at him. I held out my hand. "Let's go."

We walked around the building so we could cut across the empty lot. The Dumpster at the back door was filled to the top, and there was a pile of stuff stacked beside it. Broken things, damaged things that no one could use. It made me mad that people thought it was okay to donate crap. There was a baby mattress with the foam sticking out, two plastic chairs with the seats cracked up the middle and some kind of a stand on wheels with the top broken and splintered.

Wheels. I turned and walked back to the pile of junk. "Look at this," I said to Dylan.

"It's broken."

"I know." I tipped the stand sideways to look underneath. Yes! The sides had been screwed on. So was it okay to take it? Should I ask or just pick it up? I stood there trying to make up my mind when the back door opened and a man came out carrying a table that was missing a leg.

He smiled at me.

"Excuse me," I said. "Is all of this garbage?"

"'Fraid so," he said.

I pointed at the stand. "Would it be okay if I took that?"

He shrugged. "Sure." He reached over and lifted the stand away from the Dumpster, setting it in front of me. "I don't think you can glue the top," he said. "I think you'll need a whole new piece of wood."

The bottom shelf, with the wheels, looked big enough to hold Dylan. "I don't want the top or the sides," I said.

He tipped the stand on its side and looked underneath. "That's easy enough," he said. "Just a couple of screws on each side. Want me to take them off?"

"Yes, please," I said.

He picked up the cart and carried it over to the door. We followed him. I grinned at Dylan. Maybe we had a solution after all.

The man set the stand down on the concrete floor. "Gimme a sec," he said. He disappeared around a long metal clothing rack. In a minute he was back with a couple of screwdrivers in his hand. It took him no time to get the sides off. "There you go."

I bent down and moved the wheeled platform across the floor. "That should work," I said.

"What do you want it for?" the man asked.

"I want something to pull him around on. I was looking for a wagon, but you don't have any."

He shook his head. "Nah, we almost never get stuff like that." He studied the platform for a minute. "How're you gonna pull it?"

I hadn't exactly thought about that. I rubbed my aching shoulder with one hand. "I don't know. Fasten a rope to it somehow, I guess."

He held up a finger. "Hang on." He went around the racks again and pushed a large cardboard box out from underneath with his foot. He bent to check inside, then stood up and looked around. "Kevin," he yelled.

"What?" a voice answered from the far side of the space.

"Where'd we put those straps?"

"Hooks on the back wall," the voice called back.

The man headed for the end wall of the room and was back in a minute carrying a couple of long, thin leather straps. "I don't know what the heck these are for," he said. "Some of the stuff people bring in." He shook his head.

The leather slid through the screw holes with no problem. He knotted the ends together underneath so the strap made a looped handle. Then he smiled at Dylan. "Have a seat. Let's give it a test drive."

I figured Dylan wouldn't want to, but I was wrong. He sat down, holding on to the sides with both hands while the man pulled him across the floor and back. Dylan was grinning.

The man handed me the strap. "Try it, just to be sure."

It was ten times better than carrying him. "Thank you so much," I said.

"Hey, no problem," he said with a smile. "It's a lot better than seein' that stuff end up at the dump. I'd stick to the sidewalk though. I don't think it'll go so good on the gravel."

I nodded and thanked him again.

I didn't have to pull on Dylan's arm to get him across the lot. Now he was pulling on me, keen to get back on his train, as he called it. We made it back to the room without a problem. I thought about going back out with the laundry. My shoulders hurt, and I had a blister on the bottom of my right foot. I sat on my "bed" and watched Dylan pull Fred back and forth, and then Q was home with pizza for supper. Dylan had to show him how the train worked, so the pizza got a ride to the bathroom and back.

The pizza was cold, but so was the bottle of water Q had brought along. I'd rather eat cold pizza than drink warm water.

"Leftover from lunch?" I asked.

Q was beside me on the bed, his long legs stretched across the floor. "Yeah, some of the guys ordered it. I rescued this before it went in the garbage. Water too."

Dylan was giving Fred another ride. "He needs milk," I said. "And we don't have any way to keep it."

"Can you just buy a little thing of it for him, like at lunch?" Q asked. "By the way, what did you do for lunch?"

I took out one of the apples, and he pulled out his knife and gave it to me. "Bag lunches at St. Paul's," I said. I leaned across Q's legs and gave a chunk of apple to Dylan.

"I like his train."

I cut another chunk of apple and gave it to Q. "I had to do something," I said. "He's too heavy to carry, and when we were going to St. Paul's, he wouldn't walk."

Q reached for his jacket and pulled something out of the inside pocket. "Here," he said.

It was a bag full of pennies. Maybe five dollars. "Where did you get this?" I said.

"Some of the guys play Texas Hold'em at lunch. It's only for pennies. But I got lucky. Why don't you use it to get milk for Dylan?"

Dylan had given up on the train for now and was trying to get the bag full of blocks open. Q crawled over to help. I stayed where I was. I was glad to have the money to get milk for the kid, but five dollars' worth of pennies was heavy. And how could I pull him to the grocery store and back and get stuff washed and go get a library card?

My shoulders hurt. The blister on my foot had bled through my last pair of semi-clean socks.

Dylan was making a tower out of the blocks. It looked in danger of falling down at any second. Q slid back along the floor and reached for the bottle of water. He looked over at me, then set the bottle down and swung around, putting both hands on my bent knees. "What is it, Maddie?" he asked.

"How is this going to work?" I said. "How do we take care of him and get enough money to get out of here?" Then I said the thing that had been in the back of my head all day. "Maybe we made a mistake."

Q shook his head. "No, we didn't," he said, keeping his voice low so Dylan wouldn't hear. "He was living in a van with four other people. With a piece of shit for a father. I promise this is one hell of a lot better."

"I suck at this," I said, rubbing the back of my neck again. "I got pissed off at him. I pretty much dragged him up the street by one arm."

"And you made sure he had something to eat and you got him toys. You didn't hit him."

"No," I said.

"You didn't just leave him somewhere and walk away."

I'd thought about it for a second, but I hadn't done it. I shook my head.

"Q, c'mon," Dylan called.

Q squeezed my knees. "You're about a hundred times better than what he'd get in foster care. We're going to get out of here. It's okay. I have a plan." He went back to Dylan then, just in time for the tower to sway and fall over. I didn't want to give Dylan to someone who wouldn't take care of him. I looked at the blocks all over the floor. That's what my life felt like right now, pieces all over the place.

eleven

Doing stuff with Dylan was a lot harder than doing stuff by myself. He got tired. He got bored. He got annoying. It was work sometimes not to scream at him. The "train" was a help, but I still had to pull it. I had to figure out lunch every day. I started buying little cartons of milk at a gas station convenience store a couple of blocks away. It was a lot easier than walking to the grocery store every day, and they didn't seem to mind the pennies. Every few days, Q usually had more of them.

One day he came home with a book about poker. The cover was torn, and some of the pages were curling like they'd gotten wet. Q held up the book with a grin. "Only cost me a quarter," he said.

For a second, I wanted to grab the book from his hand and smack him with it. I still hadn't gotten to the library. I missed my math books. But that wasn't Q's fault.

A couple of days later, after we'd eaten—it was a fancy hotel-food night—Q said, "I gotta go back out."

"Goddard's making you work in the dark?" I said.

"No. I'm going to play poker."

There were so many things I wanted to say, but Dylan was right there, playing with Fred in a tent we'd made from a blanket and the broom handle.

"We have to pay for this place tomorrow," I said finally.

Q was lacing up his boots. "I know," he said. He stopped, reached into his pocket and handed me five twenties. "Here. Hang on to that, and you don't have to worry."

"I didn't mean I thought you'd lose the money," I said. Okay, so that's what I had thought, but now it seemed pretty crappy to say so.

He finished tying his boot and stood up. Dylan was inside the tent. Q wrapped his arms around me and pulled me against my chest. "Maddie, I'm good at this," he said. "I play the guys at lunchtime and I win way more than I lose. You know that."

Based on the bags of pennies, that was right.

"I need to work up into some of the games with higher stakes. It could be our way out of here, our house in the country. A different life."

I didn't want a house in the country. That was what Q wanted. I wanted to go to school. I wanted to be a doctor, although I didn't think much about that anymore. "What if you lose?"

His smile was cocky. "I'm not going to lose. But you've got the rent money, so we're safe." He glanced over his shoulder to make sure that Dylan couldn't see, and then he kissed me on the mouth. "For luck," he said.

He let go of me, poked his head in the tent to say goodbye to Dylan and then he was gone.

I put Dylan to bed, but I couldn't sleep. I cranked the radio and listened to it for a while. I kept going to the door to watch for Q. Finally I went out on the landing so I could see down the stairs to the street. I left the door open so I could hear Dylan if he woke up.

I'd been leaning on the railing for a few minutes when someone unlocked the bottom door and started up the stairs. I was about to go back inside when I saw that it was a woman, maybe about as old as my mother. She had curly brown hair sticking out from under a baseball cap, and she was a bit shorter than me. She was carrying two cloth shopping bags filled with food. I wondered where she'd been grocery shopping so late.

She smiled at me and set the bags down. "Hi," she said. "I'm Lucy. I live at the end of the hall."

The only other people I'd met had been old—two women and a man. They gave me timid smiles when we passed on the stairs, but that was it. Seeing them always scared me. Would I still be here when I was old?

"I'm Maddie." I knew Q thought we should keep to ourselves, but I just didn't want to tonight.

"The little guy with the blond hair, he's yours, right? Your brother?"

She made "your brother" a question, and I nodded. I didn't look old enough to be Dylan's mother, and I couldn't exactly say no, his parents abandoned him in the parking lot at the mall.

Lucy reached down into one of the bags and held out a large jar of peanut butter. "If you keep it between the windows, it'll stay cool but you can still spread it."

I shook my head. "No. I can't take your food."

"I have a ton of stuff," she said, still holding out the peanut butter. Then her expression changed. "Oh, hey, don't worry. I didn't pay for it."

"You stole it?" I blurted.

She laughed. "No. I'm a scavenger."

"You mean you go through the garbage?"

She nodded. "Uh-huh."

When I'd stayed at Pax, there were some people doing that.

Lucy held out the peanut butter again. "Take it, please. It wasn't even in the garbage. It was in a box on the ground. I have four jars."

"Why would somebody throw away peanut butter if there was nothing wrong with it?" I asked.

"Look at the label."

I took the jar, turning it so I could see the front. "It's upside down."

"Uh-huh."

I tipped the bottle over. It wasn't dirty, and the plastic seal was still around the lid. "That's stupid," I said.

She nodded. "I know."

I glanced at her bags again. They were filled with food.

"Look, it's all good stuff," she said. "I'll show you." She bent over the bags and started taking things out: lettuce, packaged and washed; sealed bags of tiny carrots; little round tomatoes; a carton of soy milk; the jars of peanut butter; a bottle of orange juice; four wrapped sandwiches.

I thought about what Dylan and I had had for lunch— cheese and crackers, a banana, juice boxes. I looked up at Lucy. "Stores just throw this stuff away?"

"Pretty much. Vegetables, fruit and whatever packaged stuff that's gotten to the expiration date. End of the day, they toss it out."

"So is it okay to eat?"

Lucy shrugged. "All I can tell you is that I've been eating like this for over a year and I haven't been sick once. The expiration date doesn't mean that's the day when the food suddenly goes bad." She snapped her fingers. "Like that. It just means it'll taste best before that day."

I glanced behind me. There was no sound from the room behind me. Dylan was still sleeping. "How do you know where to go?" I asked.

Lucy unzipped her jacket and leaned against the stair post. "There's a bunch of us who go out together—maybe a dozen people if everyone shows up. Over time we've figured out the best places and the best times. You should come with us sometime."

"Could I?"

"Sure. We usually go Monday and sometimes Thursday. You can come with me next Monday night if you want and you don't mind walking."

"I don't mind walking," I said. "What time?"

"Meet me here at quarter to nine," Lucy said. She picked up her bags. "Don't worry about bags. I have lots." She started down the hall. "See you Monday," she said over her shoulder.

"Monday," I said. I took the jar of peanut butter and went back into the room. Q said he had a plan. Well, now, so did I.

I was asleep when Q came in. When I woke up, he was sprawled on his air mattress, asleep and half dressed. He smelled like beer and sweat.

I gave Dylan apple slices with peanut butter. The third time I had to climb over Q's legs, I "accidently" tripped over them, which woke him up. He sat up, rubbing his face with a hand.

"You smell bad," Dylan said.

Q smiled at him. "Yeah, I'm sorry about that." He reached for his jacket, holding it upside down. Change came raining out of the pockets, bouncing on the floor and the air mattress.

"Wow!" Dylan shouted. There were dozens and dozens of quarters all over the room. He started picking them up.

"What's this?" I said to Q.

"I won," he said, getting to his feet and heading for the bathroom. "Do whatever you want with it."

Dylan and I gathered the money. I showed him how to make piles of four so I could count it all. There was thirty-five dollars and seventy-five cents.

"Maddie, are we rich?" he asked.

"Well, we are today," I said, giving him a hug. I was already thinking about where we could go for lunch.

Q played poker again on Saturday. This time there was more than forty dollars in quarters. He smelled pretty much the same as he had after the first game.

Monday night, I was waiting for Lucy at the top of the stairs. When I'd told Q what I was going to do, he'd made a face. "Oh, c'mon, Maddie. It's not so bad we have to eat food from the garbage."

"It's not garbage," I said. "Lucy had good stuff—carrots, milk, tomatoes."

"That she got out of someone's garbage."

"No. That someone carried out of the store and then she picked up. If I bought the same stuff and came out of the store and gave you the bag, you'd eat it. So what's the difference?"

He glanced toward the bathtub, where we could hear Dylan splashing. "I won more than forty dollars on Saturday. If you want milk and carrots, you can buy them."

I was starting to get pissed. I could feel a knot tightening in my chest. "What I want to do is go with Lucy and see what she does," I said. I grabbed my jacket, stuck my head around the open bathroom door and told Dylan I was going out to try to get him more peanut butter. He'd been eating it with everything. "I'm going," I said.

"You're coming back, right?" he said, his face serious. He was getting less clingy as the days went by.

"You bet," I said. "I'll bring you and Fred a treat."

That made him smile.

"See you," I said to Q and went out to wait by the stairs.

When Lucy came down the hall, she was carrying a bunch of bags. She gave me a couple of cloth bags and three plastic ones. "You got gloves?" she asked.

"No," I said. "But it's not that cold."

She smiled. "No. I meant plastic gloves."

"I thought you said you didn't actually go through the garbage."

"I don't," she said. "But sometimes things like milk cartons or yogurt containers break." She pulled a pair of thin plastic gloves out of her pocket. "Here."

I took the gloves and shoved them in my own jacket pocket. I thought about what Q had said, that things weren't so bad that we had to eat stuff out of the garbage.

Lucy walked fast. We headed across town in the general direction of the university. About four blocks over, as we waited to cross the street, she pointed ahead to a group of people—maybe five or six of them—standing on the next corner. "That's everyone else," she said.

"They won't be mad that you brought me?" I asked.

She looked at me like I was crazy. "Why would they be?" she said. "There's always way more food than we can all use."

"Hey, guys, this is Maddie," she said as we got to the others. Everyone smiled and said, "Hi." They all looked like university students except for one man in dark-rimmed glasses. His hair was dyed yellow, and he had an accent I couldn't figure out.

We walked maybe another three blocks and then the yellow-haired guy said, "Perfect timing."

At the corner, a guy in jeans and a long apron was carrying plastic garbage bags to the edge of the sidewalk. Everybody stopped. The same guy carried out three more bags. As soon as he'd gone back inside, we were moving again.

Lucy pulled on her gloves, lifted a bag away from the pile and opened it. She shook her head. "This one is garbage." She closed the bag and handed it to the guy behind her who set in on the sidewalk away from the other bags.

Yellow-hair had a second bag open. "Got it," he said. He pulled out two bags of sealed packages of salad stuff and handed them to me. "Just lay them out on the sidewalk."

I made a row of bags along the curb. There were eight all together. On the front of the bags it said, *Washed and ready to serve*. After that there were bags of little carrots and chopped up peppers.

"I've got yogurt," Lucy said. She had another garbage bag open and was handing big plastic tubs to a girl with blue hair.

"I've got sandwiches," someone else called.

Once all the food was spread on the sidewalk, Yellow-hair and a guy with a messy beard carefully set the remaining garbage bags in a pile. Lucy passed around a bottle of hand sanitizer. I took off my plastic gloves and cleaned my hands.

Everyone pretty much just took what they wanted—or maybe it was needed—and it all seemed to work out fair. I got a bag of lettuce, one of carrots and a big tub of strawberry yogurt. Someone had found apples. They looked a little bruised, but I took two anyway. Lucy handed me a jar of peanut butter.

Yellow-hair looked at his watch. "We'd better get going," he said.

We started up the sidewalk, and the girl with blue hair ended up walking beside me. "Hey," she said. "I'm Alicia."

"I'm Maddie," I said.

"Kind of surprising how much gets thrown out, isn't it?" she said.

"Yeah," I said. "Do you do this all the time?"

She nodded. "I couldn't afford to get my degree, otherwise." She smiled and kind of shrugged. "Well, I couldn't eat and get it."

"Do you get all your food this way?" I asked.

"Pretty much. And my clothes and stuff."

"Clothes?"

Alicia nodded and brushed a clump of blue hair back from her face. "Clothes, a monitor for my computer, dishes. Lucy found an iPod last week."

"Wow."

"Yeah. You should come with us next week. It's end of term, and Friday is garbage day. There'll be good stuff on Thursday night."

At the front, Lucy and Yellow-hair had stopped walking. After a minute they saw whatever they were looking for. It was another pile of garbage bags. We were outside a small bakery. I ended up with a bag of different rolls and four cookies. People were saying goodnight and heading off in different directions.

"Hey, Lucy, bring Maddie on Thursday night," Alicia said. She waved at me and headed up the hill with Yellow-hair in the direction of the university.

"You wanna come?" Lucy asked.

"Umm, yeah, I guess," I said.

She shifted her bag from one hand to the other. "You won't believe the stuff that gets thrown away at the end of term." She shook her head in disgust. "Most of them are just too damn lazy to pack stuff or even take it to the Salvation Army to donate it. It's easier to stick it out for the garbage truck."

"Thanks for bringing me," I said.

"You can come every week if you want," she said.

I was pretty sure I wanted.

"We have to get ice," Lucy said.

"For what?" I said.

"You don't have a cooler, do you?" she asked.

I shook my head. "No."

"We'll find one on Thursday," she said. "I have three. I'll lend you one. Stuff like the yogurt and salad stuff lasts better if it's cold."

We got ice at the grocery store, forty-nine cents for a big bag because they wanted to get rid of it. "They clean the machine on Monday night," Lucy explained.

When we got back to the building, she got me the cooler, a red-and-white thing like people took on a picnic, and showed me how to pack it with ice and my yogurt and lettuce. "Eat this stuff first," she said. "Everything else will last longer."

"Thanks," I said.

"No problem," she said. "Six thirty on Thursday."

I nodded, and she headed down the hallway.

I slipped into the room. Q and Dylan were asleep. I put the peanut butter in the window. Everything else was okay. I got cleaned up, brushed my teeth and put on the T-shirt and sweatpants I slept in. Dylan was making those little kid snoring noises he made when he slept. If I was lucky, I had a couple of hours before he woke up from a nightmare. He was going to be real happy about the peanut butter and the cookie.

I rolled up in my blankets, suddenly so, so tired.

"Find anything good in the garbage?" Q asked quietly in the darkness. He rolled toward me.

My good mood was gone like that. "It wasn't garbage." Okay, so technically it was garbage we were opening, but the food had been put in bags in the store and then carried out, and we got it. If the food had been in plastic grocery bags Q wouldn't be asking me such a stupid question.

"Maddie, I meant what I said before." He reached out and touched my arm. "You don't need to do this. I can work more time if I have to, and I'm pretty damn good at poker."

I didn't know how to make him understand that I needed to do this. Ever since Alicia had told me that scavenging was how she could go to university I couldn't stop thinking about it. All Q talked about was the house in the country we'd have someday. I didn't want to live in the country. I didn't want to milk cows and teach Dylan about growing carrots. I wanted to learn things and someday be a doctor. And I wanted Dylan to go to school.

"If you don't want to eat the stuff I got, you don't have to," I said. "There's nothing wrong with it, and you might as well know I'm going back out again." I rolled over. He didn't say anything else, and neither did I.

"Can you be here by six thirty for sure?" I said to Q as he got dressed Thursday morning.

"Why?" he said.

"Because I want to go out with Lucy. It's the end of term or something at the university, and she says people throw out a lot of good stuff."

"Yeah, well, forget it," Q said. "I'm playing poker."

"So play another night."

He pulled his T-shirt over his head. "I can't. This is a lot higher stakes that the quarter games I've been playing in. They don't let new guys in very often."

"I can't take Dylan with me," I said.

He reached for his sweatshirt, checked to make sure Dylan was still brushing his teeth and pulled me against him.

"I keep telling you, you don't have to go picking through garbage. I mean it." He kissed the top of my head. "See you tonight." He called goodbye to Dylan and was gone.

I still had half a bread roll sitting on the window ledge. I pounded the roll into crumbs with my fist, pretending it was Q's head. Then I ate all the little bits. I probably shouldn't have felt better, but I did.

Just before six thirty, I told Dylan to go pee and wash his hands. "Why?" he asked.

"Because we're going on a treasure hunt."

He zipped into the bathroom, did his stuff and came hopping out on one foot. "Can Fred come?" he asked. "Fred likes treasure hunts."

What the heck, I figured. "Sure," I said. "Stick him in my backpack."

Lucy was just coming down the hall when we came out. "Is it okay if I bring him?" I asked. I showed her my makeshift wagon. "I can pull him, and if it's not okay, well then... that's okay." Crap! I sounded lame.

Lucy smiled. "Sure, bring him along." She leaned down. "I'm Lucy," she said.

"I'm Dylan," he said. "And Fred is in the backpack."

Lucy frowned and looked up at me.

"Bear," I said.

She nodded and looked at her watch. "We better get going."

We clomped down the steps. Outside on the sidewalk, I set Dylan's train down and he climbed on and grabbed the sides.

"That is extremely cool," Lucy said.

We headed in the direction of the university. "What kind of stuff will there be?" I asked.

"You name it, you'll probably find it," Lucy said. She was wearing her hair off her face, pulled back with some kind of stretchy headband. "Franz—the tall guy with the black-framed glasses—he found a TV at the end of winter term. Got some detergent, some dishes, that cooler I loaned you. I think Alicia got some chairs for her place."

She tipped her head back toward Dylan. "One of the residences is for students who have kids. You'll probably find some toys and stuff for him."

The same group of people was waiting when we got to the university. Alicia smiled and came over. "Hi," she said to Dylan.

"Your hair is blue," he said.

I frowned at him. "That's rude, kiddo," I said.

He got that stubborn look on his face. "But it *is* blue," he said.

"That is so neat," Alicia said, looking at the wheeled platform. "Could I pull him?"

My arms were tired from hauling him all the way up the hill. "Uh, sure," I said, handing over the strap. The others were already headed toward some buildings. We followed, Alicia making horse sounds, which made Dylan laugh.

There were two big green Dumpsters at the side of the first building we stopped at. They were so full, the covers couldn't even close. Yellow-hair—Franz—climbed up on the side and started handing things down to the others—a black wooden chair, a desk, something that might have been a DVD player. The desk looked like it was brand-new.

In the end, I got some dishes, laundry detergent, two boxes of Pop-Tarts, a small folding table, a windup train for Dylan and, the best thing of all, a cooler on wheels.

"I'll get your cooler for you," I said to Lucy when we'd gotten everything upstairs. She'd carried my folding table, and Dylan had held her bottle of detergent on his lap.

I unlocked the room, hoping Q would be stretched out on his bed.

But he wasn't.

"Thanks," I said to Lucy.

She smiled. "It was fun." She felt in her pocket. "Here." She handed me a lime-green iPod. "The music all seems to be French."

"Are you sure you don't want it?" I said.

She nodded. "Yeah. I already have one. Would you believe all Spanish music?" She picked up her detergent bottle. "If you want to come Monday, it's the same time as last week."

"Yeah, I'll try," I said.

"See you," she said. She waved at Dylan. "Bye, Dylan."

"Bye, Lucy," he said.

The only way I could get Dylan in the bathtub was to let him set his train on the top of the toilet tank. He went to sleep with it set beside his bed. I had a fast bath and washed my hair. I tried to wait up for Q, but I was just too tired. I woke up when he came in and banged into my new table.

"Oh, Maddie, hey, I'm sorry I woke you up," he said.

It took me a second to realize there was someone behind him. I got up, wrapping the blanket around me. "Q, who is this?" I said.

He looked back at the person standing by the door. "His name is Leo," he said.

"What's he doing here?" I asked. I didn't really care if Leo knew that I was pissed.

"It's okay," Q said. "He's just here for tonight."

Dylan moved in his sleeping bag behind me. "Why?" I said.

Q didn't say anything. I took a step toward him and slugged his arm. "Why?" I repeated.

"I kinda won the kid in the game."

Kid?

I hobbled to the bathroom and flipped on the light. I could see that the person standing by the door was just a kid, older than Dylan, eleven or twelve, maybe. He looked thin and scared, his arms crossed over his chest.

"What do you mean you won him?" I said to Q.

He rubbed his face. Even with the distance between us, I could smell that he had been drinking. "It's complicated," he said.

"So uncomplicate it."

He took a step closer to me. "We'll figure something out in the morning." He lowered his voice. "He doesn't have anywhere else to go."

I looked over at the kid, who was edging toward the open door. I thought about all the scary things that were out there on the dark street. I thought about all the scary people. I went over to him. He took a bunch of steps backward, bumping into the door frame.

"Your name is Leo?" I asked.

He nodded. He was skinny, like he hadn't been eating enough.

"You hungry?"

He gave an indifferent shrug.

What did I have for food? An apple. Peanut butter. Some juice. The boxes of Pop-Tarts from tonight. Q had knocked the Pop-Tarts on the floor when he'd bumped into the new table. I bent down to pick them up. "How about a Pop-Tart?" I said. I took one out of the box and held it out to Leo. He hesitated and then took it from me. He made me think of this old dog that used to hang around Pax House— jumpy, hungry, but it wouldn't come close enough most of the time to get food.

"Come in," I said. He looked from me to Q. I couldn't see his face clearly with just the bathroom light on, but he seemed scared and at the same time trying to pretend he wasn't.

"I'm not doing stuff," the kid said. "Not with him and not with you."

Just like that old dog, he was about to run and maybe I would have let him, except I got it then, what he meant about stuff. "You don't have to do anything with anyone," I said. I pointed at Q. "Not him. Not me. Nobody. Got it? That's not how we do things."

I turned around and gave Q a shove. "You stink," I said.

He went into the bathroom and closed the door. All we were left with was the light from the street coming in through the window. It was enough to see the kid, Leo, still by the door.

I could taste something sour at the back of my throat. What kind of person bet a kid in a poker game? "Leo," I said softly. "Come in. No one's going to touch you, I swear."

He took a couple of steps into the room. I moved around him to shut the door. Then I handed him a bottle of juice. "Eat something," I said.

I leaned against the wall, still half wrapped in my blanket, while he ate. He watched me and the bathroom door. I gave him a second Pop-Tart, and he ate that too. Okay, so where was he going to sleep? The only space was in front of the door. That meant he might take off, but maybe if he felt he could go, he wouldn't.

I dragged Q's air mattress across the floor, setting it by the door and put one of his blankets on top. "You can sleep there. No one will touch you. No one."

He stood there, arms wrapped around himself, and I figured he'd just take off the second I moved. "If you want to go, you can," I said. "But if you want to stay here, it's safe. Better than out there in the dark. And you can have breakfast in the morning." I didn't know what else to say. I'd never managed to get the dog at Pax House to come to me, and one day it just stopped hanging around. Was I doing the same thing all over again?

Leo moved toward the door, and I held my breath. Slowly he sat down on the mattress, pulling the blanket around himself. Q came out of the bathroom then.

He looked at the space where his mattress had been. Then he looked at me, stretched out on my own bed. He wasn't stupid enough to try and sleep with me. He rolled up in his blanket on the floor, folding his arm under his head for a pillow.

I watched Leo sitting there in the darkness for a long time. He was still sitting there when I fell asleep.

I figured Leo would be gone when I woke up, but he was still by the door, slumped over sideways, asleep. I went into the bathroom, and when I came out, he was standing by the door, the blanket neatly folded on the air mattress.

"Hi," I said, finger-combing my hair. "You hungry?"

The shrug again. I handed him two of the plates we'd found last night and a knife. "Wash these, please," I said, jerking my elbow in the direction of the bathroom. "There's stuff for washing dishes and some paper towel in there." I figured he'd either do it or he'd go, and I needed to know which it was going to be.

He did it. I used Q's folding knife to cut up an apple. I broke a blueberry muffin pretty much in half and got juice for him and water for me.

Leo came out of the bathroom and handed me the clean dishes. I spread peanut butter on the pieces of apple and made a plate for each of us. "Here," I said. "Let's go sit on the stairs so we don't wake these guys up."

I sat on the top step and set my plate on my lap. Leo stood there for a moment. I started to eat. He leaned against the wall by the top of the stairs and slowly slid down into a squat. I watched him out of the corner of my eye as we ate. He had dark hair that fell into his eyes, which were blue. The knuckles on one hand were scraped like he'd been in a fight, and there was a bruise, almost faded, on the side of his chin. He never stopped watching, looking around, looking for what I didn't know, but I'd seen Q do the same thing.

I figured after breakfast I'd take him to Hannah. She'd know what to do. I wouldn't tell Q until after, because he'd start with his foster-care speech. And maybe he was right, how the hell did I know? But I couldn't take care of Dylan and this kid and me. There wasn't enough space. There wasn't enough food. There wasn't enough anything. And I was just starting to maybe figure out a way that I could go to school. I couldn't be somebody else's mother; I already had Dylan to look after.

"You wanna get cleaned up?" I asked when he finished eating. He didn't stink exactly, but he didn't smell great either. We went back inside. Q was awake, sitting on my air mattress and eating a Pop-Tart. I gave Leo a towel and pointed to the bathroom. "You can have a bath if you want. The door locks from the inside."

"Thank you," he said softly. He took the towel and his battered backpack and closed the bathroom door behind him.

I waited until I heard the water running before I walked over to Q and kicked him. "What kind of a stupid poker game was that?" I said.

"I'm not going back."

"He's just a kid, Q," I said.

Q's face turned serious. "Why do you think I tried so hard to win him? What was I supposed to do? Huh? I didn't know it was going to turn out the way it did."

Q needed a shave. He still didn't smell that great, and his hair was sticking up weirdly on one side, but I wasn't mad anymore. "You couldn't...you couldn't leave him, I get that," I said. "Just please don't play with those people anymore."

"How were things at the dump?" Q asked, a smile pulling at his mouth.

"Fine," I said.

"You took Dylan."

I picked up his blanket and started folding it. "I kinda had to, since you weren't here."

He sighed. "You're going to keep doing this, aren't you?"

"Yeah, I am," I said, tossing the folded blanket onto the mattress. "It's good stuff, and it's just going to end up in the garbage for real."

Dylan woke up then. While he showed Q his train, I got his breakfast ready. Leo came out of the bathroom as I was spreading a blob of peanut butter on the last of the apple. His hair was wet, and he was wearing different clothes. I pointed at Dylan. "That's Dylan," I said.

"Hey, kiddo," I called to Dylan. "Here's breakfast. Pee and wash your hands. And…and this is my friend Leo."

Dylan padded to the bathroom, watching Leo all the way. I offered Leo another Pop-Tart. He glanced toward the bathroom. I shook my head. "He won't eat one. He's on a peanut butter kick."

Dylan came out then and walked over to me for his plate. He threw his arms around my legs, and I hugged him, pushing his hair back from his face. "Can we go to the swings today?" he asked. If we went to the park, we could do the soup line for lunch. Not my favorite place, but it would be hot and not junk. "Okay," I said. "But we have to go to the laundry."

"Can I bring my train?" he asked.

"Sure," I said. "Now go eat."

Leo had watched us the entire time. I bent down to look in my stash for something for my own breakfast. When I stood up, he was gone.

"Dylan, where did Leo go?" I asked.

"I dunno," he said.

I leaned across the table to look out the window in time to see the kid run across the street. I pressed my lips together so I wouldn't swear in front of Dylan.

"He took off," I told Q when he came out of the bathroom.

"Shit!" he said under his breath. "I was afraid of that." He looked at his watch. "I have to go."

I handed him a Pop-Tart and a chunk of apple. He leaned over to kiss me, catching the side of my mouth. "See you later."

Dylan and I were on our way to the Laundromat when I saw Leo out of the corner of my eye, across the street. Dylan was being the little pain in the ass he could sometimes be. I needed the wheels for one bag of laundry, which meant he had to walk. I was carrying another bag and holding him by the hand. He had the stupid train—I had pretty quickly realized it was a bad idea to let him bring it. The bag fell off the cart for the third time at the exact moment that Dylan sat down on the sidewalk and said he was too tired to walk anymore. I'd figured out pretty quickly that snapping at him just made it worse. The only thing I could do was take one bag of dirty stuff back to the room.

I set down the bag I was carrying and reached for the one that had rolled onto the sidewalk.

"I'll get it," Leo said.

I hadn't seen him come across the street. I pulled a hand back through my hair. "Thank you."

He picked up the plastic garbage bag and looked at Dylan, still sitting on the pavement, stubbornly driving his train around his outstretched legs.

"I could carry this," Leo said. "You could pull him, I mean, if you want to."

What I wanted was to make Dylan walk, because it wasn't that far and I was mad. But that would have been stupid.

I blew out a breath that made the wisps of hair around my face fly into the air. "Yeah, that would help," I said. I pulled the wheeled platform the few feet to where Dylan sat. "Get on," I said. "And hold on tight to that train, because if it falls off I'm not stopping for it."

He smiled at me. "Yes, you will," he said. He knew when I was full of crap.

I shook my head and tried to look stern. "No, I won't."

Dylan nodded. "Yes. Yes. Yes."

"No. No. No," I said. Considering that he was always dropping something and I always went back and got it, it was a stupid argument. But it made him laugh.

We walked a block answering each other back and forth until he did let go of the train—probably on purpose—and I did stop to pick it up, and then we both laughed.

When we got to the Laundromat, Leo carried the bag inside for me and set it on an empty washer. "If you want to throw any of your stuff in, you can," I said as I started sorting. "If you want to."

I didn't look at him because I just had a feeling that if I did, he'd take off. After a minute he opened the old canvas pack he carried and dumped his stuff into the washer.

Then he fished in his pocket and handed me two quarters. It felt weird to take the kid's money, but I did.

I dropped into a chair by the window, where I could keep an eye on the washers and Dylan, who was driving his train around the bank of machines. Leo leaned on the wall by the dryers. After a few minutes he walked across the room and pulled a flyer off the end wall. He leaned over a washer. I couldn't see what he was doing with the paper. Finally he straightened. Somehow he'd turned it into a small ball. He bent down to Dylan and said something. Dylan nodded, and the ball went into the back of one of the train cars. In a few minutes another flyer turned into another ball. A third one became a bird that Dylan flew around the room. By the time everything was dry, Dylan was getting whiny again.

"We'll take this stuff home and then we'll have some lunch and go to the park," I told him.

Leo had stuffed his clean clothes into his backpack. When I tied the top of the second bag of laundry, he took it from me. I carried the other bag and pulled Dylan like before. Leo walked beside him, and Dylan talked pretty much the whole way. When we got back to the building, Leo brought the bag upstairs.

"Have lunch with us," I said.

He shook his head and took a step backward. "No. I can't," he said.

"Please, please, please," Dylan begged.

Suddenly I didn't want to do the soup line. I still had a bunch of quarters.

Maybe I could score a leftover pizza at Pizza Man. "Pizza," I said, hoping that would convince him.

"Yay!" Dylan cheered, hopping around the room on one foot.

"Okay," Leo said.

We walked over to Pizza Man, and for once Dylan didn't complain. I stood in line at the takeout window with my bag of quarters, hoping they'd have a missed pickup. They did. They had two of the small personal pizzas. One was bacon and pepperoni and the other was veggies. For the price of one, I got both.

We took the pizza to the park, sat on a bench by the swings and ate. We probably spent an hour on the swings and the climber after lunch. Finally I pulled a plastic garbage bag out of my backpack. "C'mon," I called to Dylan.

"What are you doing?" Leo asked.

"Collecting returnables," I said as Dylan raced up with a wine bottle.

"Is this good?" Dylan asked.

"Very good," I said. He tore across the grass toward the big maple, where we usually found as many as a dozen empty beer bottles.

Leo spotted two wine-cooler bottles. With an extra set of eyes, we got the bag filled pretty quickly. Leo took it, and I let Dylan climb up on my back for the ride to the recycling center. When I turned around from the counter with the money, Leo was gone.

"Hey, kiddo, where did Leo go?" I said.

Dylan shrugged. "He said he had to go."

I piggybacked Dylan all the way home, hoping Leo would just appear again out of nowhere, but he didn't.

thirteen

Q came home with food from the hotel—chicken, rice, a salad with fancy lettuce. "This is our last meal from there," he said. "Kevin got another job."

We'd been getting stuff about twice a week from the hotel kitchen. I wondered what would happen to the food now, and I was really glad I'd met Lucy. I told Q about Leo spending part of the day with us.

"I wish he'd just stayed here," he said. "He shouldn't be wandering around by himself."

"Maybe he'll come back," I said. I didn't know if it was what I wanted or not. Dylan liked Leo, and I didn't want him to have any more people who just disappeared from his life. He never said a word about his mother or his brother and sister, but sometimes he'd sit up in the middle of the night, crying and shaking. He wasn't exactly awake, but he wasn't quite asleep either. Pretty much all I could do was hold on to him until it stopped. Suddenly he'd be asleep in my arms. I'd lay him down and usually spend the rest of the night watching him. In the morning it would be like it hadn't happened.

After we'd eaten, Q got the poker book out of the pocket of his jacket and went to sit by the window where the light was best.

"What're you reading about?" I asked. "The rules of the game?"

He shook his head. "Strategy. I figured it wouldn't hurt if I could learn more about odds and stuff."

I figured it wouldn't hurt if Q just stopped playing poker all together, but I kept that to myself. That night, after Dylan was asleep, Q and I had sex again. I'd given up on it ever being the way it was in books. It was okay and all, being so close to Q, but I'd always figured it would be special somehow, and it was just…ordinary.

Monday morning I was taking Dylan to the thrift store to look for shoes when I realized Leo was behind us. I stopped and pretended to tie my shoe. Dylan looked around the way I figured he would and caught sight of Leo.

"Leo!" he yelled, a big grin lighting up his face.

Leo walked up to us.

"I'm going to get shoes," Dylan said. "You come."

I didn't wait for Leo to answer. I handed him the leather strap so he could pull Dylan up the sidewalk.

We found a pair of sneakers for Dylan. When we came out, we headed for the library, and Leo just seemed to get pulled along. I decided to try Pizza Man again for lunch. No pizza this time, but I did manage to get an order of macaroni and cheese with ham that hadn't been picked up. The three of us ate it out of the foil pan with plastic forks, sitting on the same bench in the park as we did before. This time Leo disappeared while I was pushing Dylan on the swings. I thought I saw him when I was walking back with Lucy that night, loaded with a bag in each hand because it had been a good night. I looked across the street and then back over my shoulder, but he wasn't there.

I packed the cooler and put two jars of peanut butter in the window, but once I lay down, I couldn't get to sleep. Dylan was curled up in a tiny ball in his sleeping bag. Q was sprawled on his stomach, one arm thrown over me.

When I heard the noise, the first thing I figured it could be was a mouse. It was that kind of scratching sound. Then I heard it again, and something made me get up. My heart was pounding, and there wasn't really any reason to go and look, but I had to do it. I pulled on my boots before I opened the door, because if whatever was out there was small and furry with a long tail, it was going to get its ass kicked.

It took me a second to see him in the faint light in the hall. For a second I thought it was a bag of clothes someone had dropped at the top of the stairs. Then I saw that it was a person, and a moment after that…oh God…it was Leo.

I ran to him. His face was bloodied. I touched him, and he flinched. "You're okay, you're okay," I said. "Don't move." I ran back into the apartment, grabbed Q and shook him awake. "Q, it's Leo. It's Leo. He's hurt." I grabbed one of my blankets.

Q followed me out. "Oh shit," he said when he saw Leo.

I knelt on the floor and wrapped the blanket around him. Q crouched beside me. "What happened?" he asked.

"I don't know," I said. "I heard a noise. It was him." Leo's face was swollen and dark with bruises. "You gotta find a phone," I told Q. "We have to get an ambulance."

"No!" Leo whispered, his voice low and scratchy. He tried to get up.

I knew we would all be in a mess if an ambulance came, because police would come too, but that didn't seem to matter. Leo was still trying to get up.

"Help me get him inside," Q said.

"No," I said. "He needs an ambulance and a doctor." I got to my feet. If Q wasn't going to get help, I would.

He grabbed my arm. "What he needs is to get out of this hallway, and so do we, in case whoever did this shows up."

"Fine," I said. We half dragged, half carried Leo into the room and got him on my mattress. The whole thing woke Dylan up.

"Maddie?" he called out. I heard the fear in his voice.

I kneeled by his bed. "I'm right here, kiddo."

He rubbed his eyes. "What are you doing? You woke me up."

"I'm sorry," I said. "Lay down and go back to sleep."

He squinted across the room. "Maddie, why is Leo on your bed?"

My heart was racing in my chest. Lie or truth? "Leo fell down," I said. Lie. "He got a bunch of owies."

"You can fix them, right?"

I nodded. Lie, again.

He reached down, pulled up his blanket and handed it to me. "Leo can have my blankie," he said.

The back of my throat got tight, and I had to put a hand on my chest to remind myself to breathe. I took the blanket and leaned over to kiss him. "Thanks, kiddo," I whispered.

One arm came up and around my neck. "I love you, Maddie," he whispered back.

I hugged him tightly. "I love you too," I breathed against his neck.

He rolled over and snuggled down into his sleeping bag. I set Fred over his head.

Leo was half sitting on my air mattress, slumped against the wall. I tucked Dylan's blanket around him and went for some water and a towel. Q caught my arm. "No ambulance, Maddie," he said in a low voice. "He'll run."

I shrugged off his hand. "I know," I said. I put warm water in a little plastic bowl I'd gotten at the thrift store for a quarter. Then I got the only clean towel we had and knelt on the floor beside Leo. I dipped the end of the towel in the water and started cleaning his face. He shook, and tears mixed with the blood and dirt on his face, but he didn't make a sound. I didn't even try not to cry. I wiped at the tears and dipped a clean end of the towel in the water.

I could sense Q standing behind me. "The bag of quarters is in my jacket pocket," I said. "I need Band-Aids and some kind of cream with antibiotics. And aspirin." I didn't turn around to look at him. "There's an all-night drugstore somewhere. I don't know where."

And I didn't care. That was his problem. I knew about the all-night drugstore because Hannah had gotten stuff from there one time when I was staying at Pax House and a woman had shown up with her kids after her husband had banged her face into a cement block wall about twelve times.

I heard Q pull on his clothes and get his jacket and boots. He touched my shoulder as he went past me, but he didn't say anything and neither did I.

It took a long time to clean Leo's face. His left cheek was scraped raw. There was a gash over his eye and another cut in his hair. His right eye was swollen shut. Even though I couldn't see them, I knew there had to be bruises. And there was gravel and other crap stuck to his skin.

I threw the towel in the bathtub—it was ruined. Then I got a bottle of water from the cooler, glad that I'd listened to Lucy when she'd pushed me to grab a couple of the bottles we'd found with the wrapped sandwiches at the bakery.

I put the bottle in Leo's hand. He took a drink, coughed and took another and then another.

When Q came back, he had some kind of anti-everything cream in a tube, plus gauze pads and tape. I put cream on most of Leo's face and the back of his right hand and I used the tape to stick one of the gauze pads on top of the cut by his eye. That was all I knew how to do, and I probably wouldn't have known that if I hadn't been at Pax the night that woman came in. I sent a thank-you to Hannah out into the universe.

Leo needed to see a doctor. And I knew that wasn't going to happen. Leo would run. Q was right about that.

Q rolled up his jacket and made a pillow for Leo. Then he made a bed for me on his mattress, rolling up in a blanket on the floor beside it. We didn't talk at all, but when I reached out into the dark for his hand, I found it.

I wanted to run. I thought about it, about sitting up, getting my boots and my backpack and taking off. Q said that foster care was worse than being on the street. But was it? Was this better for Dylan? It wasn't better for Leo. Being here was better than wherever he'd been, but was it better than getting off the street altogether? If I went, Q wouldn't have any choice. He'd have to at least take Dylan somewhere.

Then I thought about Dylan's arm sliding around my neck. If I disappeared, what would that do to him? And what about Leo? I knew in my gut, in a way that I couldn't put into words, that if I was gone Leo would be too. Maybe he'd take off before morning anyway, but I knew he'd run if I did.

I stared at the window. Was the right answer in here or out there? I slid my hand out of Q's. He sighed in his sleep. Then I heard another sound.

Leo was crying—so softly that if I hadn't been awake, I wouldn't have heard him. The sound made my throat tighten and my eyes swim with tears. I didn't move because I didn't know what I should do, and then for some reason I remembered the first time Evan hit me. He struck me across the face with the back of his open hand so hard that I went over sideways in my chair onto the floor. I cried that time. It was the only time I cried. The second time I got even, and the third time I got away. But the first time, I cried, and no one came. No. One. Came.

I crawled over to Leo and took his hand. He jerked the way he always did when someone got close, but I didn't let go. I laced my fingers in his and held on just as tight as I could. After a minute I slid next to him, my shoulder against his and my back against the wall. I wiped my own tears away. We sat there like that for a long, long time.

I couldn't let him take off. Which meant I had to stay too. "Wanna know a secret?" I said softly. "I'm afraid of the dark. Stupid, huh?"

"No," he whispered after a moment.

"My dad, he always said there's nothing there in the darkness that isn't there in the light." He had, and when he'd been alive, it had been true, and if he was still alive, it would probably still be true, but he wasn't and it wasn't. "But that's not true, Leo," I said. "There's bad stuff in the dark and bad people, and it's just better if we stick together."

He didn't say anything.

"So don't take off, okay? Stay with us. I won't let anybody hurt you, and you don't have to do anything you don't want to do. Just please don't..." I didn't know what else to say.

The moment between us got longer and longer and longer. Finally Leo whispered just one word into the darkness: "Okay."

He fell asleep after a while, and I went back to my mattress. Q was sprawled on the floor with his mouth hanging open. Dylan, like always, was curled into a little ball like one of those fuzzy caterpillars. Leo slept the same way. I watched all three of them. I watched them sleep for a while, and I knew that they were my family now. I thought about being a doctor one last time, and then I put the idea away, the same way I had with all the memories of my dad, because it was just better not to think about some things.

Leo was still there in the morning. His face was bad. Nothing looked infected and nothing seemed to be broken, but I was just guessing.

Dylan stared, and I was just about to send him in to wash his hands when he crawled over to Leo. "Does it hurt?" he asked.

"Yeah, some," Leo said.

Dylan thought about that for a minute. "Are you going to stay here?" he said.

Q was just coming out of the bathroom. "Yes," he said. He jerked his head toward the open door behind him. "Go get ready for breakfast," he said to Dylan, who smiled at Leo and crab-walked to the bathroom.

Q turned to Leo. "I'm not going to ask what happened last night because I'm pretty sure you wouldn't tell me. If you stay here with us, nobody will touch you. You wanna help out, that's good, but you don't have to do anything you don't want to. Okay?"

Leo nodded. "Okay."

We had breakfast, and I was glad the haul from last night had been so good. After Q left, I got the food organized. Everything was easier with Leo around. I wondered if he had a little brother or sister; Dylan was bugging him all the time, but he never got mad.

We went to St. Paul's for bag lunches to add to what I'd gotten from scavenging. Leo kept the hood of his sweatshirt up, and it hid the worst of his face.

"How did you get all this food?" Leo asked. We were in the park again. Dylan was hopping around the bench pretending to be a rabbit because it was the only way I could get him to eat salad.

I told Leo about meeting Lucy and about all the food that got thrown out. "You can come sometime, if you want," I said. "Nobody asks any questions."

Dylan had hopped his way over to the slide. "Are you and Q a couple?" Leo asked.

I'd never really thought about that, which was weird, considering we'd had sex and Q had said he loved me more than once. "Yeah, I guess we are," I said. "But most people think we're brother and sister, and I let them."

"Why?"

I shrugged. "I don't know. I just do."

Dylan waved from the top of the slide, and I waved back.

"He's your little brother, right?" Leo said. "Not Q's."

I shook my head. He was part of the family. He deserved to know the truth. "His parents left him, well, his father anyway." I told him the story.

"They didn't come back? You're sure?"

I kicked a dented tennis ball across the grass. It looked like it had been chewed by someone's dog. "They didn't come back. There's a guy Q knows up there who works maintenance at All-mart, and he's been watching for them. And Q's been back too, probably five or six times." I shot a quick sideways look at Leo. His face was starting to look better already.

"Is anyone looking for you?" I said.

He closed his eyes for a second and shook his head.

"Are you sure?"

He wouldn't look at me. "I have bad in me," he said. "I shouldn't be around you, or Dylan, or anybody."

"You don't have bad in you," I said, not even trying to keep the anger out of my voice. "And whoever told you that is full of shit."

He didn't say anything.

I got in his face because everything I'd been feeling was suddenly coming out as mad. "You think there's bad in Dylan?" I asked. He was going down the slide feet first on his stomach. "His family just left him, left him, in the parking lot at All-mart."

Leo shook his head, but he still wouldn't look at me.

I couldn't stop. It was all spewing out of me now. "And what about me? Is there bad in me?" It was the first time I'd actually said it out loud, because sometimes I thought maybe it was true. Maybe Evan was right, and maybe I was going to burn in hell. "That's what my mother's boyfriend said. He said I was going to burn in hell forever. You think he's right, huh? You think he's right?" Bits of spit were spraying out all over the place.

"No!" Leo looked at me then. "You're not bad and neither is Dylan. They're bad."

I knew he meant Evan, and Dylan's parents.

"Then you can't be bad either," I said. I swallowed a couple of times. "The bad is in the person who hurt you." All the anger had turned into something else all of a sudden, and I thought I was going to start crying. I blinked like crazy because I really hated girls who cried at everything.

"I can't go back," Leo said. We were back to not looking at each other again.

"Yeah, well, you can stay here," I said. I knew for sure then that I didn't have to worry about him running anymore.

Q came home with another air mattress and a blanket for Leo. I didn't ask him where he got the money, but he hadn't given me back the bag of quarters. He'd also gotten a deck of cards. He sat on the floor by the window after supper shuffling through the cards and reading his poker book.

I watched him for a while. I could tell he was frustrated by the way he kept yanking his hands back through his hair. Finally I went over and sat beside him. Leo was building a tunnel for Dylan's train with the wooden blocks.

"It's just a game, Q," I said.

He let out a breath before he answered me. "It's our best chance of getting a house and getting out of here."

"We'll find some other way."

He did the hair-hand thing again. "What other way?" he said.

I leaned back against a stack of boxes. "I don't know. There has to be something."

"I'm good at poker, Maddie," Q said. There were black circles under his eyes, and he hadn't shaved this morning. "I just need to know more about how to figure the odds." He stretched his arms out to the sides. "It's so friggin' boring."

"So let it go for tonight."

"I can't."

"Yes you can," I said. "I'll give you a chocolate chip cookie. Fresh from the garbage."

He shook his head at me, trying not to smile.

"C'mon," I said. "Yummy, yummy garbage cookies. You know you want one." I rubbed my stomach.

That made him laugh. He closed the book and set it up on the box. Then he leaned back beside me.

"Lucy's friend, Franz, sells stuff he finds," I said. "At this flea market they have in the mall on Sunday afternoon. Maybe we could do that."

Q rested his head against mine, and when Leo and Dylan weren't looking, he kissed me on the side of the forehead. "Yeah, and how much does he make? Fifty bucks?"

"I'm not sure."

"There are some high-stakes games out there. Kids at the university, where Mommy and Daddy are paying for everything. One win at one of those games and we'd be set. All I need is to work on this odds stuff and get a bit more practice." He kissed my ear this time. "One win will give us everything."

Right. So what would one loss give us?

fourteen

Q played poker again on Friday night. He had another bag of quarters on Saturday morning. We went to the soup line both days for lunch. Leo was jumpy, like he was gonna come out of his skin. I wondered if he was afraid whoever smashed his face would show up. It was healing nicely. He didn't need a bandage on the cut anymore, and I just put the cream on at night.

Q helped me take all the blankets and towels to get washed. Staying even halfway clean was a lot of work. It cost money for the washers. It cost money for the dryers. Soap cost money. None of us had enough clothes that we could have clean stuff every day. At least we sort of had hot water most of the time. But the bars of soap and bottles of half-used shampoo I'd gotten at the university went way faster than I'd expected.

I was always afraid we smelled.

Monday night I was outside Whole Village dividing up half a box of small cartons of yogurt when I heard my name. Lucy looked up, and I looked around. Hannah had just crossed the street at the corner.

I stood up.

"Is everything okay?" Lucy asked.

"Yeah, I know her," I said. "I'll be right back." I walked over to Hannah.

She looked past me to where Franz was laying bags of lettuce on the sidewalk. "Maddie, what are you doing?" she asked.

"We're not breaking any laws," I said.

She touched my arm. "You don't have to eat from the garbage. Come back to Pax House."

"I'm not eating from the garbage. We're gathering food that's still good so it won't end up in the garbage."

"You don't have to do this," Hannah said.

It was so easy for her to tell me what I should do. I was pretty sure that cute sweater she was wearing hadn't been at the bottom of a bin at the thrift store. And I knew if I stepped a bit closer, she'd smell like coconut soap that probably hadn't come from a Dumpster.

"I want to do this," I said. I looked over my shoulder. Lucy had stood up and was looking at us. "I have to go."

She caught my sleeve. "Come see me tomorrow."

Lucy started toward us.

"I'll be there until eight."

"Maddie, you all right?" Lucy raised her voice so Hannah would hear.

"Maybe," I said to Hannah.

She let go, and I walked back to Lucy. "She giving you a hard time?" Lucy asked.

"She...uh..." I pointed to the bags. "She doesn't get it."

Lucy rolled her eyes. "Lots of people don't."

I really wished Hannah hadn't seen me. I was going to have to go see her now, and I didn't want to. But I didn't want her to make trouble for everyone else. What if she went to the store manager? Or what if she called the police? I didn't think she would, but it would just be easier if I went.

After we'd eaten the next night, I pulled Q into the bathroom. "I gotta go do something, and I'll tell you about it later, I swear. It shouldn't take me any more than about an hour."

"Is it another Dumpster thing?" he asked.

It was hard to stand still. I wanted to get going and get it over with. "Not exactly," I said. "But it kinda has to do with it. I'll explain it all when I get back. Okay?"

His eyes narrowed, and he studied my face for a minute. "Yeah, go," he said. "But be careful."

I made sure I had my whistle, told Leo and Dylan I'd be back soon and left. It was weird being out by myself. I always had somebody with me, Q or Dylan and now Leo, and Lucy and the others on Monday nights. I could walk as fast as I wanted. I didn't have to talk. I didn't have to listen.

I knew one of the guys at the door at Pax. Jayson. He remembered me too. Jayson had huge hands. I'd always figured there was no trouble when he was around because he looked like he could squeeze the brains right out of your head with just one of those hands. I could do it with a tomato, say, but I just had the feeling Jay could do it with somebody's head.

I told him Hannah wanted to see me. "Yeah, she said you might come by. Everything okay for you?"

Had Hannah told him she'd seen me going through the garbage? "I'm good, Jay," I said.

He held the door open. "I think Hannah's in her office."

She was in the kitchen. She smiled when she saw me. "Maddie, I'm so glad you came," she said. "Can I get you something to eat?"

I shook my head. "No thanks." I didn't usually turn down food, but I wasn't hungry and I wanted to get out of there as fast as I could.

"C'mon back to my office," Hannah said.

I followed her through the kitchen and down the hall. She dropped into one of the two black chairs on the visitors' side of her desk and pointed at the other one. "Have a seat, Maddie," she said.

I knew what this meant. This meant we were going to have one of those "friend" conversations. She'd had them with other people, not just me, and she did it on this side of the desk. I'd figured that out from listening in on stuff that was pretty much none of my business, but what the hey, I was bored a lot when I'd stayed at Pax.

Hannah would lean forward in the chair and start with, "I'm your friend." Then she'd tell you how you could fix your life in three easy steps.

I sat down, but on the edge of the seat because I wasn't going to be there very long.

"You haven't been around," she said. "How are you?"

It must have been a really crazy day, because she didn't have any lip gloss on and there was a tiny bit of something—maybe broccoli—stuck between her bottom front teeth. "I'm good," I said.

"I was surprised to see you last night."

I shrugged. Where did she expect to see me? Pushing a cart in the Superstore?

"I'm worried about you."

"You don't need to worry. I'm okay."

She leaned her elbows on her knees and laced her fingers together, kind of like she was going to pray for me. "C'mon, Maddie," she said. "We're friends, aren't we?"

Not exactly "I'm your friend," but close enough. I shoved my hands in the front pocket of my hoodie. "Not really," I said.

For a second her mouth moved without any sound coming out. Then she said, "Why would you say that?"

"Because it's true." I looked around her office. "Hannah, you were really nice to me when I was here, but that doesn't make us friends. You run Pax House, and I stayed here because I had nowhere else to go."

Silence. I waited to see if Hannah would say something, because I'd already said what I had to say.

She exhaled softly. "I care about you, Maddie," she said at last. "If you came back here, we could work things out, you could go to school, you could make—"

Work things out meant go home to my mother and Evan. I'd told Hannah I couldn't do that, but she just didn't want to believe me.

"Stop!" I stood up, both hands in the air over my head. "I get that you think I should go home, go back to school. What you don't get is it's my choice and my life."

"So you're going to live on the street forever?"

"No!"

"Then what are you going to do?" Her face was flushed.

How was I supposed to answer that? Tell her about Q's plan to win big at poker? This wasn't getting us anywhere. I knew getting mad just made things worse. When I dug in, so did Hannah, but she was the adult here. Wasn't she supposed to be reasonable? Wasn't she supposed to listen? "I have friends," I said.

"Friends who are eating out of the garbage."

"It's not garbage," I snapped. "You don't know what you're talking about."

She got up and stepped in front of me with her hands on her hips. "I know what happens to people out here, Maddie," she said, her voice sharp with anger. "People start using, or they slide down into a bottle, and then they end up doing things they never would have done otherwise. I don't want to see that happen to you."

"It's not going to happen to me."

Hannah shook her head. "Everybody says that, Maddie. You think most of the people that come through here weren't like you once?"

"Stop doing this!" I shouted, holding up one hand. "Stop trying to scare me! And stop trying to make me into you!"

I ran out of the office, cut through the kitchen and pushed through the heavy metal door to the outside. I stood there breathing hard, rubbing the back of my head with one hand.

Jayson was watching me. "You okay?" he asked.

I nodded.

"Hannah's a good person," he said.

Great, not him too. Why couldn't the do-gooders go work on someone else's life? I gave a halfhearted nod because I didn't want to get into it with Jayson.

"You doin' okay, Maddie?" he asked. "Really?" I could see concern in his chocolate-brown eyes. "You got somewhere to sleep that's safe?"

I gave him a small smile. "Yeah, I do. Honest."

"Good." He smiled back. Then he fished in his pocket and pulled out a folded sheet of paper. He held it out to me. "Do me a favor?" he said. "Keep an eye out for this kid. Runaway. Parents are going crazy."

I unfolded the page to look at the picture. The blood drained from my face, and for a second the world swirled around me. My breath stuck in my chest.

It was Leo.

I would have given it away; Jayson would have known right away from the look on my face except that somehow, just at that exact second, some smart-ass guys came down the sidewalk talking loudly, pushing each other, showing off. He turned his attention to them, folding his arms and somehow looking even bigger than usual. By the time the guys had gone by and Jayson looked at me again, I'd remembered how to breathe.

I folded the paper into a small square and stuffed it in my back pocket. Then I looked at him with what I hoped was a normal expression on my face. "What did he run away from?" I asked.

Jayson shook his head. "Nothing, far as I know. Swear to God, the parents are frantic. How often does that happen around here?" He glanced up the street where the boys had gone back to shoving each other and talking trash.

"Nobody runs away without a reason," I said.

"Doesn't mean it was a good reason." He stretched one arm behind his head and then the other. "You didn't see these people. Mother looks like she's about to cry all the time. Father's going on about two hours of sleep. They're nice people, Maddie."

I thought about Leo insisting he could never go home. I thought about the way he cringed whenever anyone other than Dylan got close to him. Nice people? I wasn't so sure.

"I gotta go," I said to Jayson.

"Stay safe," he said.

I nodded. "Yeah, you too."

I could feel the folded piece of paper in my pocket. It seemed to get heavier with each step I took. When I got home, I stopped on the sidewalk and pulled it out. Leo looked serious in the picture, but it was him, with longer and what looked to be darker hair. His parents were offering a reward. A big one. That had to mean they cared about him, didn't it? Then I thought about Leo telling me he was bad. If they cared about him, if they loved him so much, why did he think that about himself?

I folded the paper as small as I could and put it back in my pocket. Then I went upstairs.

I didn't tell Q about Leo's family looking for him. I don't know why, I just didn't. But I kept the piece of paper. I told him about seeing Hannah when I'd been scavenging and how I'd gone to talk to her because I didn't want her asking around about me.

We'd never talked much about our lives before. Q knew I'd stayed at Pax House, and he knew I'd left home because of Evan. I knew even less about him, and it didn't matter anyway.

Getting through the day was a lot easier with Leo around. We needed more food, and I was always afraid Q was going to come home and say John Goddard thought we were using too much water, but having Leo just to help with Dylan was worth it.

And he was smart. He seemed to remember everything he read. We'd carry home stacks of books from the library and, more than once, I woke up in the middle of the night to find Leo, wrapped in a blanket, reading on the bathroom floor.

Sometimes he didn't want to sleep. He had nightmares a lot worse than Dylan's. He'd move in his sleep like he was running from something, and at the same time he'd try to curl into a tiny ball. He made sounds like an animal caught in a trap—pained moans that made the hair on the back of my neck stand up.

I'd crawl over and sit beside him in the dark until he jerked awake, wet with sweat. Then I'd hold his hand until he stopped shaking, and lots of times we'd fall asleep like that. I learned pretty fast not to try to put my arms around him or touch him before he was awake. That made him freak.

Like Q, Leo was watching all the time, but when we were all together and he was playing with Dylan, he almost seemed like a normal kid. Or at least as normal as our family was ever going to get.

"Leo should go to school," I said to Q. We were sitting on the floor by the window. He was working with the cards and a different poker book. Dylan and Leo were building some kind of house for Fred.

"You know we can't do that," Q said, setting down the hand of cards he'd just dealt himself. "Schools ask a lot of questions."

"Couldn't we...fake it?" I asked.

He didn't say a thing. He just looked at me like my brain had fallen out and rolled across the floor.

I slumped back against a box. "Okay, so we can't fake it," I said. "There has to be a way. He's smart, Q."

Q reached over and tucked a stray piece of hair behind my ear. "So are you. You teach him."

I rolled my eyes. "Yeah, there's a good idea."

"I'm serious," he said. "People teach their own kids all the time. You can do it. Give me a list of what you need and I'll get it for you."

"How exactly are you going to do that?" I asked.

"Goddard," he said. "You really want to know any more than that?"

I pressed both hands to my face. "No," I muttered through my fingers.

I made a list for Q—notebooks, pencils, a math textbook, a calculator, a math set, plus crayons and colored paper for Dylan—and a couple of days later, he came home with it all in a paper shopping bag. The next Saturday he got up early.

"I have to work today," was all he said. He came back dirtier than I'd ever seen him. That was how it always was with Goddard. He always got the best of any deal.

Q played poker pretty much whenever he got the chance. As far as I could tell, he was winning more than he was losing, but I couldn't be sure. The bags of change seemed to come pretty regularly—thirty dollars, sometimes forty. Mostly he played with the guys he worked with, but sometimes he went out for what he called higher-stakes games.

I always pretended to be asleep when he came in, but I could tell by the way he moved if it had been a good night or not. If it was, he was cocky, even as he was creeping around the room. If it wasn't, he kind of crawled in and rolled up in his blanket away from me.

He read the poker book over and over, dealing cards and mumbling to himself. "What are you doing?" I asked him one night while I sorted through our food stash trying to figure out what we were going to have for breakfast.

"I'm trying to learn how to figure the odds so I know when to bet," he said.

"Don't you just bet when you have the best cards?" I asked as I shook a box of Oatios, trying to figure out how much was left inside.

He set the open book on the floor and stretched his legs out across the painted wood. "I wish it was that simple." His hair was smushed flat on one side from where he'd been leaning his head on his hand as he read.

"I think I'd rather collect bottles," I said. I stepped over him and scooped up Dylan. "Bath time," I whispered against his neck, scrambling my fingers up the back of his head to make him laugh.

When I came out of the bathroom, Q was bent over the book again, cards spread out in front of him. He picked up his pencil and scribbled something on a piece of paper next to the cards on the floor. Leo had moved closer and was watching.

Q studied the paper and then looked at the cards again. He shook his head, set the pencil down and scratched his chin. "I'm missing something," he said. "I wish I knew what the hell it is."

Leo was looking at the paper, even though for him it was upside down. "Your outs are wrong," he said softly, more like he was talking to himself.

Q looked surprised. "What do you mean, they're wrong?"

Leo pointed to the cards. "A flush is better than a straight, right?"

Q nodded. "A flush beats a straight, yeah."

Leo pushed the piece of paper toward Q. "Your outs are wrong," he said again.

"How do you figure that?" Q asked.

"Those two cards are yours?" Leo asked. There was an ace and a jack in front of Q.

"Yeah."

"Those other three are the...?"

"Flop," Q said. He pushed the cards closer to Leo, a ten and a king—both hearts—and a five of spades.

Leo looked at Q. "So if the next card is a queen, you have a straight, and if it's an ace, you have two the same."

Q tapped the deck with a finger. "Assuming no one is holding a queen, there are four to be had and three aces— since I have one. Four and three make seven, so I have seven outs. Seven chances to make my hand and win."

Leo shook his head. "No. Really all you have is five. If the queen or the ace is a heart, then there will be three hearts showing and there's a good chance someone else will—"

"—be able to make a flush, which would beat my straight," Q finished. He took a deep breath and blew it out. "How did you figure that out? I've been doing it wrong for weeks."

Leo shrugged. "It's just math."

Q picked up the poker book and started flipping through the pages. He stopped near the front and held out the book to Leo, pointing to the middle of the left-hand page. "Do you understand that?" he asked.

Leo leaned over and started reading. After a minute he looked up at Q. "It's pretty simple."

Q turned to grin at me and then bent his head over the book with Leo. I could feel the energy coming off Q in waves, while in my stomach, something cold twisted itself into a knot.

fifteen

The next night, Q started teaching Leo poker. Or maybe it was Leo teaching Q, I wasn't so sure. They were at it when I left with Lucy and were still spreading cards on the floor when I came back. At least Dylan was asleep, and judging by the mess in the bathroom, he'd had a bath.

I stepped into the middle of the cards on purpose so they'd have to stop. "Jeez, Maddie, what are you doing?" Q said.

"I'm trying to put the food away," I said. "You could help."

Leo reached for one of the bags, but I handed it to Q instead. "You should go get cleaned up and brush your teeth," I said to Leo. I saw him look at Q, who gave a slight nod.

Leo went into the bathroom and shut the door. When I heard the water running, I hit Q on the head with a loaf of French bread. (It was in a plastic bag.)

"Ow!" he said, looking at me wide-eyed.

I bent to put the bags of ice in the cooler. "Oh c'mon, that was bread. There's no way it hurt," I said over my shoulder.

He rubbed his hair just above his left ear. "What did you hit me for? What did I do?"

I glanced at the bathroom door. "Leo's a kid," I whispered. "You really think he should be playing cards?"

Q reached out to touch me, but I was pissed, so I took a step backward. "He's not playing cards, Maddie. I'm playing cards. All Leo's doing is teaching me how to figure the odds so I know when to bet and when not to." He put his free hand flat on his chest. "The only one playing is me, I swear." He waited a minute, and then he wiggled his eyebrows all spazzy at me.

I stared over his shoulder and tried to keep the scowl on my face. "That's not working."

"Are you sure? Because I think I just saw your lips try to smile." He took a step toward me.

"The inside of my cheek was itchy," I said.

He took another couple of steps toward me so there was maybe just a hand-width of space between us. "I don't think that was an itch," he said. "I think that was a smile."

"Wasn't," I mumbled. I was still staring at a spot on the wall over his shoulder, so I didn't see the kiss coming. His mouth was warm on mine. One hand was in my hair, and the other slid down my back.

"I'm lucky, Maddie," he whispered, his breath soft on my skin. "I've been lucky since the day I met you. Once I figure out when to bet and when to fold, there's nothing to stop us. We're gonna get out of here."

I looked up at his face. It seemed like there was something in his eyes, an intensity that for a moment reminded me of the minister at the Holy Rollers shelter the night Q and I met. Then it was gone. It had to be some trick of the streetlight coming through the window, because that preacher and Q were nothing alike.

Every night for the next week, Leo and Q worked with the cards and the book. Each day Q seemed a tiny bit more frustrated. I wasn't sure if Leo could see it, but I could. Q was always yanking his hand back through his hair, and the muscles in his jaw and neck looked like tight knots under his skin.

Sunday we went to the soup line for lunch. We were low on food. We'd been to the bag-lunch line both days at St. Paul's, and I'd used the last of the quarters to buy milk for Leo and Dylan.

We had granola, apples and carrots for supper. I pretended that I wasn't very hungry so there'd be enough of the cereal for Dylan and Leo to have for breakfast. Q pulled me out into the hallway after we ate. "Do you have any money?" he asked.

"If I had money, do you think we would have been eating wrinkled apples and rubber carrots for supper?" I said.

There was a long pause. "You always keep something hidden in case there's an emergency," he said finally.

I didn't know he knew that.

"What's the emergency?"

His eyes slid off my face. "There's a game tonight."

"No," I said. I turned around to go back inside.

Q grabbed my wrist. "Maddie, I need to practice."

I wrenched my arm free. "So practice with Leo."

"It's not the same as being in a game."

I had to jam my hands into my pockets because I was suddenly afraid that if I didn't, I would punch him. "So practice with those dip wads you work with. I don't have any money, and if I did, it would be for an emergency, and poker is not an emergency."

I went back inside, and after a minute Q came in too. I thought he'd be more pissed, but he wasn't. I was glad because the thing was, I'd lied. I did have money—twenty dollars, underneath the sole in my left boot. The part I didn't lie about was that it was for an emergency, and Q playing poker wasn't an emergency.

He smiled at me and started building a castle with Dylan and Leo—or maybe it was a condo for Fred. After I'd cleaned up a little, I kicked off my boots and lay on my stomach on the floor, watching them. I would have listened to the iPod, but it needed to be charged and I didn't have a charger. I hadn't understood the words, but I'd liked the French music.

When it was time for a bath, Dylan didn't want to go, even though I'd seen him yawn more than once.

"Now," I told him after he'd whined and stalled. "There isn't going to be any hot water if you don't move it. You'll be in the bathtub with icicles hanging from your ears."

I was pretty sure John Goddard had done something to the water heater. The water wasn't as hot as it had been, and lots of nights there was none at all. We'd started having baths every second day because nobody wanted to get in a tub of cold water.

When I came out of the bathroom, Leo was sitting on his air mattress reading a book about airplanes. The blocks had been put back in the bag.

"Where's Q?" I said.

Leo looked up. "He said he had to go somewhere."

He said something else. I know that because I saw his lips move, but I couldn't hear the words over the rushing sound—like waves hitting the beach—in my ears. My left boot was lying on its side by the end of my mattress. I bent and picked it up with shaking hands. Q hadn't even tried to put the insole back in properly. I felt for the twenty dollars, knowing that I wouldn't find it. And I didn't.

The boot fell to the floor, and I pressed a hand over my mouth because I thought I was going to puke up apples and carrots all over the floor.

"Maddie, are you all right?" Leo asked, touching my arm. I hadn't even heard him get up.

What should I say to him? That I was angry? That I was scared? I closed my eyes for just a second. *Suck it up*, I told myself.

I swallowed the sour taste at the back of my throat and looked at Leo. "I'm all right, I'm all right," I said.

He looked scared, his face pale.

"It's okay, I swear." I put my hand over his for a second and forced a smile I didn't feel. "Help me pick things up," I said.

He looked at me for a long moment and then pulled his hand away and picked up Dylan's blankets. I took all my fury, all my fear and stuffed it in a big mental box for now. When Q came home, I was going to hurt him. I was going to hurt him bad.

I sat outside in the hallway to wait for Q, leaving the door open a crack, in case Leo or Dylan woke up. I think I fell asleep with my head against the wall, but I woke up when Q started up the stairs.

He'd been drinking—big surprise. He smelled like beer, cigarettes and dirty bodies. I got to my feet as he got to the top step. He swallowed a couple of times, swaying a little, like a small tree in the wind.

I slapped him. Hard. I opened the box in my head where I'd stuffed all my rage at finding the money gone and let it out.

He sucked in a breath, but he didn't move. He didn't say anything. He just looked sad. Very, very sad.

"I'm sorry," he finally whispered.

"You should be!" I hissed. "You had no right to touch my stuff or take that money! What the fuck is wrong with you?"

He didn't seem to know what to do with his hands. "I thought I'd win," he said.

I was right in his face. "I don't care!" I spat. Then the words sank in. My legs went rubbery, and I felt behind me with one hand for the wall to steady myself. "You lost, didn't you?" I said.

He couldn't look at me. He stared at the dirty tile floor instead and slowly nodded.

My stomach was churning. "How much?"

He swallowed again. "The twenty dollars."

"And?"

"The rent...money."

I lifted my hand to hit him again. I wanted to pound him until he was nothing but a lump on the tile. Then I let my arm fall. What good would that do?

I took a step toward the door and then I turned back to Q. "I don't care where you sleep tonight," I said. "But you're not sleeping here."

I went inside, pushed the door shut with my body, and locked it. I slid slowly down to the floor, covered my head with my arms and cried.

By morning, I was all cried out. The rage had turned to something cold and hard inside me.

"Where's Q?" Dylan asked when he woke up.

"He had to go to work really early," I said. Leo gave me a look I couldn't read. I met his gaze, hoping I looked like I had it all together even though I didn't.

We had the last of the cereal and the last carrot for breakfast. "Get your stuff on," I said after we finished eating. "We're going out to hunt for bottles."

I'd seen flyers stuck up around town about an outdoor concert on the riverbank behind the hotel last night. I was hoping if we got over there early we could get a lot of the bottles before the hotel staff started cleaning up. We could go to the Community Kitchen for lunch, but I had no food and no money for supper.

We filled three and a half garbage bags with returnable bottles—mostly wine coolers—before a tall, gray-haired man came out of the hotel and chased us off. He would have taken the bags, but I stared him down. I don't know, but maybe he could see in my face that it wouldn't be good for anyone if he made a big deal about them.

We got less than ten dollars—a forgotten pizza and milk, if we were really, really lucky.

I caught Leo watching me more than once, his face troubled. I didn't know what he'd guessed or might have heard. I didn't even know if Q was coming back. I didn't like the idea of leaving Leo alone with Dylan, but I had to get out with Lucy or there would be no breakfast. I'd pretty much decided to take them both with me when Q came in. He looked like crap, albeit sober and fairly clean crap.

"Hi," he said. There were dark circles under his eyes and stubble all over his face.

"Hi," I said. I could feel Leo's eyes on us. I wanted to act normal, but I couldn't remember what that looked and sounded like.

Q cleared his throat. "How...how was your day?" he asked.

It was hard to look him in the face. "Okay," I said. "How, uh, was yours?"

"All right." He looked at the bags I was stuffing into my backpack. "You leaving soon?" he asked.

I nodded, doing up the zipper on the back. "You're not going anywhere, right?" I said.

"No," he said quietly. We stood there awkwardly for a minute, not quite looking at each other. "I'll get Dylan in the tub," he said finally.

I gestured at the door. "I'd better go wait for Lucy."

It wasn't exactly a smile he gave me. He turned and scooped up Dylan, swinging him upside down, teasing that he was going to wash Dylan's hair in the toilet, while Dylan laughed and squealed.

Leo was still watching me. He was doing better about being touched, at least by Dylan and me. A couple of times he'd even let me hug him. It seemed like it was a good time for that now.

"I gotta go," I said. I put one arm around his shoulder and gave him a squeeze, messing his hair with my hand.

He hugged me back, awkwardly with one hand, but he hugged me back.

All of a sudden there was a lump in my throat. I smiled at him, a real smile. "I'll be back soon," I said.

It was a good night scavenging, thank God, because I probably would have sat on the sidewalk and cried if it hadn't been. Q was waiting for me, sitting on his air mattress with just the light coming in through the window from the street. He set the ice in the cooler, and we put things away without saying a word.

"Can we talk, Maddie?" he asked as I put the jars of peanut butter in the window.

"Okay," I said. Leo and Dylan were both curled up sleeping.

We went out into the hall, leaving the door open a crack. He sat on the floor, legs bent, back against the wall. After a second's hesitation, I sat beside him, leaving a little space between us. He rested both wrists on his knees and stared down into his lap.

"Maddie, I am so, so, so sorry for what I did," he began. "I'm sorry I took your money. I'm sorry I lost everything. And most of all I'm sorry I wrecked your trust in me."

He took a deep breath and let it out. "I'm trying to fix it. I asked everybody today about extra work."

"Will Goddard give us an extra couple of days to get the money for rent?" I asked.

"I'll find a way to get the money," Q said in a flat, emotionless voice.

"That means no, doesn't it," I said.

"He's a prick," Q said. "And so am I."

I looked at him then. "You're nothing like John Goddard. You're an asshole, but you're nothing like him."

That actually got me a tiny smile. He put his hand on the floor between us. It took me a minute, but I put mine on top of his. "I am so goddamn sorry, Maddie," he whispered. "I thought I could do it. There's a game, Thursday night, on campus, big stakes. I figured I could, I could win enough to get us out of here, to give us a start." He pulled his fingers back through his unruly hair. "I'm just not Leo. My brain doesn't work that way. I can't do the calculations the way he does in his head. I can't figure out the odds. I'm lucky, but that's not enough. I can't do it."

"I can."

Leo was standing in the doorway. He looked from Q to me. "I can do it. I can win."

I got to my feet. "Go back to bed, Leo," I said. I wondered how much he'd heard. Too much, that was for sure.

"Let me go to the game. I can get us the money," he said.

I shook my head. "No."

Both hands were clenched at his side. "I can do this, Maddie," Leo said.

I kept shaking my head. "I don't care if you can do it. You're not going to a poker game with a bunch of scummy people. That's the stupidest thing I've ever heard of."

Q stood up and touched my shoulder. "Let him talk, Maddie."

I whirled around to stare at him. "Let him talk? Why, Q? We're not doing this. Did you forget you won Leo in a poker game? Won him like he was a bag full of quarters?"

Q exhaled slowly. "This is different."

I folded my arms around my body, hugging myself, because all of a sudden I was cold. "No, it's not. Poker's not our way out. It's just not." I bent down and pulled off both my boots and held them out to Q. "And I don't have any more money for you to steal."

He didn't say anything, but even in the dim light I could see his face getting red. I dropped my boots back on to the floor and turned to Leo. "We'll figure something else out. No more poker games."

Leo looked away. His mouth moved, but he didn't say anything. He just turned and went back inside.

Q slid his hands over his head, squeezing it between his forearms. "I'm not fighting you on this, Maddie," he said.

"Good," I said. "There has to be some other way."

"Yeah," he said. He reached over and slid a finger down my cheek. "You look tired."

"You too," I said.

He swung his arm over my shoulder, and we went inside.

Leo was quiet the next day. If he wasn't watching me, he was watching Dylan, but he said very little.

Q came home with leftover pizza and root beer. The cards and the poker book had disappeared. Still, there was part of me that remembered how he'd taken the money from my shoe and taken off, so I watched him. And he knew it.

He came up behind me while I was checking to see which bananas had the biggest squishy spots and quickly kissed the top of my head. "Want me to wash Dylan's hair?" he asked. "There's hot water, at least for now."

"Please," I said.

He caught Dylan around the waist with one hand and made slurpy fart noises on his arm to drown out Dylan's protests about the hair washing. Q kicked off his shoes and somehow managed to get his socks off without letting go of Dylan.

I felt myself start to relax. Q had offered to wash the squirt's hair. He hadn't left it for me and then taken off with Leo. When he'd said he was sorry about before, he'd meant it.

Dylan was wired by the time he was clean. "I'll wipe up the bathroom," Q said. "There's no point in two of us being wet." He'd rolled up his sleeves, but there was a big wet spot on the front of his jeans.

Leo started playing a game with Dylan and Fred. The teddy bear was either in the jungle or the circus. I wasn't sure which.

There was a lot of climbing, and Fred kept squeezing into places and jumping back out again to the sound of clapping. I pushed all the air mattresses against one wall and started sweeping the floor.

"Maddie!" Dylan suddenly wailed.

I spun around. Dylan pointed at the window with a shaking hand, and tears were sliding down his face. "Fred fell out the window," he managed to choke out.

I put my arms around him and looked at Leo, who looked stricken. "He pushed him through one of the holes," he said. "It's my fault."

Instead of a screen, the old window had three holes in the bottom for fresh air, covered by a piece of wood that swung up and down. I looked through the glass. The bear was lying in the street.

Q came to the bathroom door. "What is it?" he asked. He was still barefoot.

"Fred fell out the window," I said. "I'll get him."

"You sure?" Q asked.

"Yeah, you don't have any shoes on." I gave Dylan a squeeze. "Stay right here," I said. "I'm going to go get Fred. He's tough. He'll be fine."

I ran down the stairs praying some car wouldn't come and run over the stupid teddy bear before I got there.

No one did. Fred was just sitting there on the pavement, none the worse for wear. I grabbed him, brushed a bit of dirt from his furry backside and went back upstairs.

Dylan was sitting on his mattress. His face was blotchy and his nose was running. I held out Fred, and he wrapped the bear in, well, a bear hug. Then he threw an arm around me. "I love you, Maddie," he said.

The hairs came up on the back of my neck. Dylan was the only one in the room. "Dylan, where's Q?" I said. "Where's Leo?"

He looked up at me with his runny nose and dirty face. "Q had to go and Leo had to go with him and they couldn't wait, so Q said for me to sit on my bed until you came back up with Fred, and I did because I'm a good boy, aren't I, Maddie?"

My legs gave way, and I slumped to the floor with a sound like hundreds of bees buzzing in my ears. They lied. They tricked me. They planned it.

Dylan was staring at me, and I forced a smile, or at least I hoped that was what it looked like. "Kiddo, how did Fred fall out the window?" I asked. There was a lump in my throat I couldn't swallow away.

He hesitated. "Leo said it was okay if Fred put his head through that hole to look outside. Are you mad?"

I felt the sting of tears, but I blinked them away because I couldn't cry in front of Dylan. That would scare him. "I'm not mad," I said. "But don't let Fred do that again, okay?"

He nodded and wiped his nose on his sleeve. How could Q do that? How could he use a little kid? Did he think if they came back with a bunch of money that everything was going to be all right with us?

I took a couple of shaky breaths, and then it hit me. Where did they get the money? I didn't have anything else hidden anywhere. Had Q somehow managed to borrow some or get some? I pressed the back of my hand against my mouth and looked around the room. All the food was still there, and the cooler was under the table, along with my backpack.

I caught the skin on the back of my hand between my front teeth and bit down hard so I wouldn't scream. The metallic taste of blood filled my mouth. I crawled across the floor until I could reach the strap of my bag and pull it over. I felt in the front pocket with one hand. The iPod was gone.

I pulled Dylan onto my lap and held him tightly, my cheek against the top of his head. I didn't realize I was crying until I saw the tears falling onto his hair.

Somehow, I got him to sleep. He had to know something was wrong, but he didn't ask any questions, so I didn't have to lie to him.

Sixteen

I sat by the door in the dark, leaning against the boxes to wait for Q and Leo. I didn't know what I was going to say, or what I was going to do. I didn't think that far ahead. I just waited.

How much time went by, I don't know, hours for sure. It had to be. Finally I heard a sound outside in the hall. I got up.

The door swung open, and Q was framed in the dim light from the one bulb burning in the hallway. One sleeve of his jacket was torn, his lower lip was split and bleeding, and he smelled like vomit.

And I didn't care. Whatever I'd felt for Q was gone. In the hours I'd spent sitting in the dark, everything had changed. I'd changed.

"Where's Leo?" I said. My voice sounded husky in my ears.

"I don't know," Q said flatly, starting to push past me.

I stepped in front of him and put a hand on his chest. "What do you mean, you don't know? What happened?"

He looked past me, not at me. "What the fuck do you think happened? We lost the money."

The shaking started in my legs and spread through my body. "Is Leo hurt?" I said.

Q shrugged. "He took off."

I looked frantically around the room. Where was my sweatshirt? Where were my boots? Panic made me want to race out into the street and start screaming for Leo. "We have to find him," I said. "Where were you?"

He pushed my hand away and tried to get past me again.

I grabbed the front of his jacket. "What the hell is wrong with you?" I said. "We have to find Leo. He's out there, and he's probably hurt."

Q looked at me finally. "No," he said with a slight shake of his head.

The panic felt like a wave that was going to roll over my head and push me under. Behind me, Dylan made a noise in his sleep and rolled over. I pulled Q into the bathroom. He stumbled over his feet, banged into the bathtub and swore.

"Look," I said. "I don't care what happened. I don't care about the money. All I care about is finding Leo and making sure he's okay." I didn't know what to do with my hands. I couldn't seem to keep them still. They were in my hair, touching my face, pushing up my sleeves. "We'll wake up Dylan and take him with us and then, and then we can split up."

Q shook his head again. "It's over, Maddie," he said in a flat, dead voice. "All of us, we're nothing. It's finished." His hands hung at his sides.

"We are not finished," I said hoarsely. "We'll find another way to make money. We can get out of here. We can do anything. We're a family. You, me, Dylan and Leo. That's why we have to go and find him."

"Give it up, Maddie," Q said. There was something that looked a lot like pity in his red-rimmed eyes. "It was a fantasy. It wasn't real. We were never a family."

I launched myself at him, beating on his chest with my fists, punching, hitting, pushing. He just stood there and took it while I beat out my rage on him until I sagged against the sink and started to cry. Then he moved past me without touching me, without speaking, without even looking at me.

I wanted to curl up into a little ball on the bathroom floor. All I could think about was Leo out wandering around the streets, and Dylan, asleep on the floor a few feet away. I didn't care what Q said. We were still a family.

When I came out of the bathroom, Q was gone. So was some of his stuff. "Fuck you," I whispered into the darkness. Then I pulled on my sweatshirt and my boots and woke up Dylan. "Get dressed," I told him. "We have to go out."

"Maddie, it's dark. I don't want to go out," he whined.

I put a hand on either side of his face. "I know you don't," I said. "But we have to go. Leo is lost and we have to find him."

He pulled himself up straighter, and I could see the determined gleam in his eyes that usually meant I was in for some grief. "I can help find Leo," he said. "I'm good at finding things."

I blinked away tears that I'd thought were gone. "I know you are, kiddo," I said, kissing him on the forehead. "Hurry up and get your things on."

I tried to think of where Leo might go. I had no idea where the poker game had been and no way to find out, with Q gone. Before, when Leo had run, he hadn't run very far. I was hoping that, like then, he was somewhere close by.

When Dylan and I stepped into the hallway, part of me hoped Leo would be sitting on the stairs or hanging around on the sidewalk by the outside door. He wasn't. I didn't even know which direction to go or where to look first. "Which way?" I said to Dylan.

"That way," he said, pointing up the street.

It was as good a place to start as any. I touched my pocket. The long shard of broken glass was back where it belonged. If we had to walk all over the goddamned city, I was going to find Leo.

I walked for hours until it got light, pulling Dylan on his little cart. We looked in alleys and behind Dumpsters. We checked the convenience store where I bought milk and the gas bar where I used to go to brush my teeth before

I met Q. We went to the playground, and as the sun came up, we walked along the riverbank behind the hotel where we had collected bottles.

"Maddie, I'm hungry," Dylan said. He'd been so good, doing his best to help me find Leo.

"We're going to go home and have some breakfast," I said. My arms ached, and there was a gnawing pain in my stomach. Beyond feeding Dylan, I didn't know what I was going to do.

We were almost home when I felt this strange sensation. It was almost like someone was behind me, standing way too close. I looked over my shoulder. There was no one there. But...It wasn't that I actually saw movement across the street. It was more like I felt it somehow. I stopped and listened. Nothing.

I started walking again, but the feeling didn't go away.

This time I didn't stop to listen. I didn't even stop to think. I turned around, crossed the street and headed for the narrow walkway between the brick building on the corner and the next one up. A few steps into the alley, I stopped. "Leo, are you here?" I said.

There was a sound, a movement of some kind from behind a metal Dumpster filled with cardboard. I bent down and picked up Dylan so I could run like stink if it was a drunk, or a hungry rat.

But it was Leo, squeezed into the space between the wall and the end of the Dumpster. Dylan struggled to get out of my arms, and threw himself at the older boy. "Leo, we found you!" he shouted.

Tears slid down Leo's face. "Don't cry," Dylan said. "You're not lost now."

I knelt in the dirt and wiped the tears away with my hand. All I could see was a small purple bruise on Leo's cheek. "Are you all right?" I asked.

He swallowed and nodded. I wrapped my arms around him, and Dylan leaned his small, warm body against us. I sent a silent prayer of thanks skyward.

We went back to the room. Leo carried Dylan, and I pulled the wheeled cart. We had granola, applesauce and yogurt for breakfast. Dylan was wild from lack of sleep. Leo was very, very quiet. I was cold, inside and out.

After we'd eaten, I pulled Dylan onto my lap. "I need to talk to Leo for a bit," I said. "Could you play train with Fred for a while?"

"Can we go to the park after?" he asked.

I nodded.

"Can I have a cookie?"

I reached over and wiped a splotch of applesauce from his chin. "Yes, you can have a cookie."

"Can I have a cookie now?" He grinned at me.

"If you stop asking questions, yes."

The grin got bigger. He threw his arms around my neck for a quick hug and then climbed off my lap and raced over to get a peanut butter cookie from the bag on the table.

I moved over to sit by Leo. "Where's Q?" he asked in a low voice.

I felt my face tighten. "I don't know," I said.

Leo stared down at the floor. "It's all my fault."

"No, it isn't," I said. I looked over at Dylan. Fred was sprawled stomach down on one of the train cars, and Dylan was driving it around the table legs. I put a hand on Leo's arm and kept it there even when I felt him flinch under my touch. "This is my fault and it's Q's fault, but it sure as hell isn't yours."

"I couldn't do it," he whispered. "I thought I could act older and keep track of the cards and all the dumb stuff people do to give themselves away when they bet, and I couldn't." His eyes filled with tears. "I wrecked it. I wrecked it for all of us."

Dylan was sharing a bite of his cookie with Fred, who was still on the train but on his back now. "Leo, when we collect bottles, how many does Dylan pick up?" I asked.

"I, uh, I don't know. Seven or eight, maybe," he said.

"Six," I said. "I counted."

Leo pulled at a loose thread on his shirt. "He's just a little kid."

I dipped my head, tipping it sideways so he pretty much had to look at me. "Yeah. There's no way he could ever gather up enough recyclables for us to get enough money to get out of here. Just like there's no way you could win enough money playing poker. You're a kid, Leo, just like Dylan.

Older yeah, but otherwise there's not much difference. It was a stupid, stupid idea. It wasn't real."

"Is Q coming back?" he asked.

"I don't know," I said, leaning back against the wall. "It doesn't make any difference. Whatever we do, it's you and me and Dylan. No running away. Okay?"

I couldn't see his face. I kept my hand on his arm and waited out the silence. And then, finally, he said, "Okay."

After lunch we took Dylan to the park. Leo chased him all over the play climber, and I pushed him on the swing until my arms were two pieces of floppy spaghetti.

For supper we had sandwiches and salad. There was no money for milk, but I had a small container of soy milk that was still cold from the remnants of the ice. After we ate I methodically searched the room, hoping I'd find a bit of change, a forgotten twenty-dollar bill or something of Q's I could sell. I didn't find anything.

I sat up most of the night trying to figure something out as I watched Dylan and Leo sleep, but there were no answers in the dark. This was real, and like I'd told Leo, there wasn't going to be any running away.

In the morning we ate some of the yogurt and the last sandwich in the cooler. The ice had melted, and I knew the last couple of containers of yogurt weren't going to be any good.

I packed the peanut butter, the bread, apples and cereal into my two shopping bags. All the blankets, the sleeping bag and our one clean towel went into one of Q's boxes. I piled his things neatly on his empty air mattress. Mostly I went from one chore to the other without thinking beyond that.

"Are we leaving?" Leo asked.

"Yes," I told him. "The landlord will be here at lunchtime for the rent for next week, and I don't have any money."

He exhaled softly. "Where will we go?"

"I don't know yet," I said. "I'll figure something out."

There was too much to carry, I realized, and I couldn't leave the food or the blankets behind. "Leo, would you take Dylan and go out and find us a grocery cart?" I said. "There's always some around the gas bar." I knew he wouldn't run if he had Dylan with him.

He hesitated for a moment and then turned to Dylan. "C'mon, squirt," he said. "Let's go."

I stacked all the things we couldn't take along one wall, and then I swept the floor and cleaned up the bathroom. I didn't really know why it was important to leave the place clean, but it was.

Before the boys came back, I walked down the hall and knocked on Lucy's door, but she wasn't there. I went back to the room for a piece of paper and a pencil. I didn't know what to write. I settled for *Thank you for everything*, and signed my name. Then I slipped the paper under her door.

We took two bags of food, the blankets, a garbage bag with a change of clothes for each of us, Dylan's toys and the school stuff. We didn't really have room for the books, but I wasn't leaving those behind.

We ate lunch down by the river. I would have gone into the library for a while, but we couldn't leave the shopping cart.

Once it started getting dark, we headed along the street in the direction of the organic foods market. I'd noticed an old building being renovated along there that had a garage in the back. The house was boarded up and surrounded by a chain-link fence, but the garage was open and we went in.

It was piled with stuff that had obviously been saved from the house—wood trim, a fireplace mantel, a chandelier—but it was fairly clean and completely dry.

"Maddie, I wanna go home," Dylan said.

I crouched down beside him. "I know you do," I said. "But we have to stay here for tonight."

His lower lip wobbled. "Fred doesn't like it here."

"Do you think he would feel better if he had a cookie?" I asked.

He nodded slowly. I fished in the bag of food, found the cookies and gave him the biggest one.

Leo was prowling around the back of the garage. "Maddie," he called. "I found some boxes."

I eased my way around a pile of wood. Leo had found several flattened cardboard boxes piled by the back wall of the garage. I spotted what looked like a blue tarp on the floor. "Bring that too," I said, pointing.

Using the tarp and the cardboard, we made a little lean-to in one corner of the garage. It was pretty much the only thing I remembered from being a Brownie, other than how to make s'mores.

I put Dylan in his sleeping bag in between Leo and me. The plastic tarp and cardboard trapped our body heat, and it wasn't really cold at all. Dylan fell asleep with his head on my lap.

I dozed off for a few minutes and then woke up with a jolt, unsure of where I was. It was dark outside, just a little light coming in through the dirty window on the opposite side of the garage. I looked over at Leo. His head was tipped back against the blue tarp, and he was staring into the darkness.

"Hey," I said softly.

He turned his head to look at me. "What are we going to do?" he whispered.

"I'll figure something out," I said quietly.

"If we go to a shelter, they'll ask a lot of questions."

"I know," I said. "It might not come to that."

"I'm not going back, not ever," he said, his voice low and rough with anger.

I reached across Dylan and found Leo's hand, holding it tightly in mine. I wanted to say I understood, but how could I? I wanted to say it would be okay, but how could I do that either?

"He said...he said no one would believe me if I told," he whispered.

"I believe you," I said fiercely, tightening my grip on his hand.

"He said he would hurt my mother…and I knew he could do it." I could feel the tears sliding down my face.

"And…and ruin my dad."

Ruin my dad? Oh God! Oh God, it wasn't Leo's father. My breath stuck in my chest. It wasn't Leo's father who had…

"Leo, who…who hurt you?" I managed to choke out.

"My grandfather," he whispered.

I could feel the folded-up flyer in the back pocket of my jeans. I'd held on to it for some reason I couldn't explain to myself. They were looking for him. They cared about him. They loved him. And if I told Leo, our family really would be finished.

I reached over Dylan, still sleeping, with my free arm and pulled Leo into a hug. He put his head on my shoulder and cried. And so did I.

seventeen

We were awake and out of the garage before any of the workmen showed up, and we'd put the tarp and boxes back neatly against the end wall of the garage. We pushed the cart to the park. I used a knife to pop the lock on one of the bathrooms so we could all pee and wash our hands. Then I wiped up the sink and relocked the door behind us.

We had cereal, yogurt and water for breakfast. I wondered where Q was waking up. He'd made his choice, and I was making mine. Dylan took Fred and raced over to the slide. Leo got up to go with him.

"Hang on a sec," I said. My heart was pounding so hard, it should have banged its way out of my chest. I pulled the paper out of my back pocket and handed it to Leo.

He frowned. "What is this?" he said.

It was hard to look at him, but I made myself do it. "Just…just look at it," I said.

He unfolded the page and stared at it. His hands started to shake, and so did the paper. He looked up at me.

"Nothing was your fault, Leo, nothing," I said. "It's all your grandfather. He's evil…he's…garbage. They love you. They've been looking for you all this time."

He shook his head.

"Yes," I said. I pressed a hand against my mouth for a moment so I could get my breath. "I should have told you, and I'm sorry I didn't. But…but…they love you. I promise they do."

He looked at me, stricken. "But I love you," he choked out. "And Dylan. You're my family. You need me, Maddie. I want to stay with you." He crumpled the flyer into a ball and threw it on the grass.

I grabbed his arm. Both of his hands were squeezed into tight fists. "Sit," I said, pulling him down onto the bench beside me. I looked over to where Dylan was going down the smallest slide with Fred on his lap, and then I turned back to Leo.

"You need me," he said, his face tight with stubbornness. "I can help you with Dylan and we can collect more bottles and I can get a job and we can make it work."

"Stop," I said. "Let me talk." I took a deep breath and let it out. "Leo, you and Dylan, to me it's like I'm your mom, not your big sister, your mom, and I know that sounds weird because I'm not that much older, but that is how it is. I love you two more than anything in the world."

"We're a family, so we stay together," he said.

I looked skyward for a second and then back at him. "I'm not done," I said.

He nodded but didn't say anything.

"Do you know what it was like when I didn't know where you were?" I said. "It felt like a piece of my heart had been yanked clean out of my chest. If you ran away again, it would be like that all over again. Every bite of food I had would make me wonder if you had enough to eat. When I lay down at night, I'd wonder if you had somewhere safe and warm to sleep.

"And I'd look for you. I'd walk the streets day and night. I'd look inside every building in this city. I'd stop every single person on the sidewalk and ask if they'd seen you. As long as I could breathe, I'd look for you."

My eyes filled with tears. "That's how your mother and father feel," I whispered. "That's what they're doing."

He swallowed a bunch of times, trying to keep his own tears down. "You don't know that for sure."

I put both hands on his shoulders and forced him to look at me. "I do know that for sure," I said. "I know what's in her heart because you're my child too."

"I'll never see you again, or Dylan," he whispered.

"Yes, you will," I said, reaching up to cross my heart with one hand. "I promise."

Dylan was at the top of the slide again with Fred. He waved at us, and I waved back.

"He deserves better," I said. "Better than a father who would leave him in the parking lot at All-mart with a stranger. Better than sleeping on a cardboard box and collecting bottles along the riverbank. He deserves a house and a yard and a dog and a swing set. He deserves a real bed and shoes that didn't come from the garbage. And so do you."

Tears slipped down his cheeks, and his nose was running. He wiped his face with the end of his shirt. "Now?" he asked.

"Yeah," I said.

"I'll get Dylan," he said. He started across the grass, then stopped and ran back to me, throwing his arms around me. "I love you, Maddie," he whispered.

"I love you too," I whispered back.

I watched him walk over to Dylan. This was the right thing to do. I knew that. What I didn't get was why the right thing had to hurt so much.

We left the cart in the park. I put Dylan's toys in my backpack, and we left everything else behind, just the way we were leaving that life behind. I carried Dylan all the way to Pax House because I didn't know if I'd ever get to do that again.

Jayson was on the door, and he didn't even ask me what I wanted. He held open the door and said, "Hannah's in her office."

I shifted Dylan's weight so I could carry him with one arm, and I took Leo's hand with the other.

Hannah was at her desk. I stopped in the doorway, and she looked up. The color drained out of her face. She came around the desk.

"Maddie, what do you need?" she said.

I wanted to run. I really did. But I was done running—for Leo, for Dylan, for me. I met Hannah's gaze without any tears. "Help," I said.

eighteen

Foster care was everything Q had said it would be and none of what he'd said it would be, all at the same time. Somehow Hannah had pulled strings, or maybe she had a picture of someone important with a goat, but she managed to get Dylan and me placed together.

My mother had told the judge she couldn't manage me, so I couldn't go home. I'd seen her once since that day in court. I didn't hate her. She just didn't have what it takes to be someone's mom—not mine, not anyone's.

We got to see Leo every second Saturday. In two months he'd grown about three inches. He wasn't on guard the way he used to be, always watching, watching, watching, and he didn't shrink if someone touched him. His grandfather was in jail. He'd probably rot there—Hannah's words not mine, but I liked the sentiment.

The first time I'd seen Leo's mother, I'd half expected her to yell at me or slap me. Instead she'd laid her hand on my cheek and smiled. "Thank you for taking care of Leo," she'd said.

I think I would have liked it better if she'd yelled.

I always pasted on my happy face when we saw Leo. I was happy to see him, and I didn't want him to know how much I hated foster care. No one had been able to find Dylan's family. Eventually someone would be able to adopt him. I knew that would be the best thing for him.

No one was going to adopt me. First of all, I was too old. And second, I had an attitude problem. That's what I'd heard Joanne, our foster mother, tell the social worker on one of her visits. She said I was angry and sarcastic and didn't know how to be a kid.

I'd cop to the sarcastic, but I wasn't angry. What did I have to be angry about? And I did know how to be a kid. I was just way past that after everything that had happened.

Joanne didn't like the fact that I put Dylan to bed every night. You'd have thought she'd be glad she didn't have to do it. At least once a week, she offered. I'd just shake my head and say, "No, thank you." I wasn't giving up Dylan. He needed me.

I always washed out the bathtub while he brushed his teeth so I could have a few more minutes with him. I was putting toothpaste on the brush when Dylan looked up at me and said, "Maddie, is it wrong to like Joanne?"

"No, it's not wrong," I said, slowly.

"'Cause I still love you. And so does Fred."

"I love you too, kiddo," I said, kissing the top of his head. "And Fred. Now brush your teeth."

Once Dylan was in bed, I went into my room and sat on my bed in the dark. I didn't want Dylan to think he had to pick between Joanne and me. I didn't want to do that to him. Like Leo, I wanted him to have a family that loved him, and that just might be this one.

When the house went quiet, I got my old backpack down from the closet. I found my whistle and the piece of broken glass.

I walked around all night, on kind of a visit to how things used to be. I stood in front of the building we'd lived in and looked up at the window of our old room. That made me think about Q. I hoped he'd find a way to get his house in the country someday. I probably should have been mad at him, but I wasn't anymore.

I walked by the organic foods market and the bakery and wondered if Lucy and the others were still scavenging on Monday nights. I spent a lot of time in the park, just sitting on the bench at the edge of the playground. I could almost see Dylan chasing Leo around the swings and flying down the slide with Fred on his lap.

I ended up at the library, sitting on my favorite bench and watching the sun come up over the river. That's where Hannah found me.

She sat next to me without saying a word. We watched the sun rise in silence, and then she nudged me with her knee. "Talk to me, Maddie,'" she said.

"What if I don't have anything to say?"

"Then I'll have to do all the talking. Is that what you want?"

"I'm running away," I said. I didn't look at her.

"Yeah, I kind of guessed that part," Hannah said. She stretched her legs out in front of her. "It's not fair, you know."

"What's not fair?"

"You running away. Dylan and Leo, they need you."

I shook my head. "No, they don't. No one needs me anymore." I looked at her then. "You know what?" I whispered hoarsely. "It was better when we were all together and eating food out of the garbage."

"It wasn't garbage," she said softly. "And it wasn't better. Otherwise you wouldn't have showed up in my office with those kids."

Something in her face changed. She slid down until she was sitting on her heels and then stared out at the river. "I have an idea," she said finally. "Promise me you'll go back and you won't run away again until you hear from me. It shouldn't be more than a couple of days."

I kicked a rock and sent it skidding across the grass. "Why should I?"

"Because if you run away again, I'm just going to hunt you down and we'll have another long conversation like this and you know you hate that. Plus I might be able to help, and what the heck do you have to lose?"

I stared at the water. It was as flat as a mirror. "Why are you doing this?" I asked.

"I'm just a natural, know-it-all, meddling do-gooder," Hannah said with a smile.

She was right about that.

The next day when I got home from school, Hannah and my social worker were at the house. I stood in the doorway between the kitchen and the living room.

"Come sit down," Mrs. Thomas, the social worker, said.

"I'm fine here," I said.

I waited for the lecture about my attitude, about how I needed to get along, about how I was a bad influence on Dylan.

Instead, Mrs. Thomas smiled at me and said, "We've decided you're not going back to school."

Was this supposed to be my punishment? Because it was a really lousy one. I hated school. I didn't fit in and I wasn't ever going to.

But it wasn't a punishment. Mrs. Thomas had arranged for me to study for and write the GED exam instead of going to school. It turned out that Joanne was a teacher, and she would tutor me in the morning.

I didn't know what to say. I'd been such a pain in the ass, I couldn't believe she was going to do that for me.

The social worker went over the details, and then Joanne walked her out to her car. I leaned against the door frame. Hannah was standing by the sofa. She'd gotten to her feet when Mrs. Thomas had gotten up. "You work hard in the mornings and get your GED, and you could start university in January," she said.

"So what happens in the afternoon?" I asked. January was too far away to think about.

Hannah walked over and smiled at me. "In the afternoon you'll be going to help at Grace House."

"What's Grace House?" I'd been waiting for the catch, the punishment. Maybe this was it.

"Grace House is a foster home for babies who have been born to alcohol-and-drug-addicted parents," she said. "They need a lot of love. It seems to me you might have some to spare."

I went to Grace House the next afternoon. I wasn't sure if it was a punishment or a keep-Maddie-from-running-away thing. The front door was opened by a young woman in yoga pants with her hair pulled into a ponytail on top of her head. She was holding a very small baby in blue sleepers. She smiled and said, "Hi, you must be Maddie. I'm Claire."

I could barely hear her, the baby was screaming so loudly. I nodded, and she handed me the baby. "This is Jesse," she said. She turned and went back into the house. I followed her, holding the baby under his arms, out in front of me.

Claire was already headed for the playpen in the middle of the room, where another baby was pulling himself upright.

Baby Jesse was screaming even louder. He kicked his legs, and I realized one of them was in a cast. The image of Leo lying in the hall, bruised and bleeding, flashed into my mind.

I folded my arms around the baby, pulling him in against my chest, against my heart. His face was red and wet with tears, and his screams rang in my ears.

I remembered all the times Dylan had thrown his arms around my neck.

I remembered holding Leo's hand as he told me about his grandfather.

I whispered softly to the baby. I don't even know what I said. I rocked him slowly from side to side and finally, unbelievably, he stopped crying.

He lifted his head and looked at me. I kissed the top of his head and breathed in his baby smell. He laid his cheek against my chest and closed his eyes.

And slowly, slowly, I felt his warmth settle into my heart.